T0407279

WINTER
BY
WINTER

Jordan Stratford

WINTER BY WINTER
Copyright © 2019 Jordan Stratford. All rights reserved.

Published by Outland Entertainment LLC
3119 Gillham Road
Kansas City, MO 64109

Founder/Creative Director: Jeremy D. Mohler
Editor-in-Chief: Alana Joli Abbott
Senior Editor: Gwendolyn Nix

ISBN: 978-1-947659-96-4 (Print),
ISBN: 978-1-947659-60-5 (eBook)
Worldwide Rights
Created in the United States of America

Editor: Gwendolyn N. Nix
Cover Illustration: Chris Yarbrough
Cover Design: Jeremy D. Mohler
Interior Layout: Mikael Brodu

Printed and bound in the United States of America.

Visit **outlandentertainment.com** to see more,
or follow us on our Facebook Page
facebook.com/outlandentertainment/

Hew wood in wind, sail the seas in a breeze,
woo a maid in the dark, for day's eyes are many.
Work a ship for its gliding, a shield for its shelter,
a sword for its striking, a maid for her kiss.

– Hávamál 81

For the shield-maidens. You know who you are.

With thanks to Chris Humphreys for his Viking library, to Ian Sharpe and Josh Gillingham, to Heather Schroder for her early read and note to "smell the herring", and to Dr. Jón Karl Helgason for his clarity and insight. And to Zandra for everything, always.

"There were once women in Denmark who dressed themselves to look like men and spent almost every minute cultivating soldiers' skills... They put toughness before allure, aimed at conflicts instead of kisses, tasted blood, not lips, sought the clash of arms rather than the arm's embrace, fitted to weapons hands which should have been weaving, desired not the couch but the kill."

— The Danish Histories of Saxo Grammaticus,
12th Century

I remember giants from the earliest of times, they who raised me long ago. Nine worlds I remember, the nine great realms hanging from the world-tree, all beneath the earth.

A tall ash-tree, Yggdrasil, sprinkled with the white waters, from which come all the dews of the valleys, stands evergreen above the Well of Urd.

And to this tree come three wise maidens from the pool beneath. One maiden is called Urd, the other Verdandi, and the third Skuld. Past and present and future, together they carved the runes, issued laws, and gave orleg—fate— to the children of men.

— PART I —

A swan. Whiter than the mist, though dappled with red and orange. That's the fire's light reflected in her feathers. She swims on, calmly.

It's still morning. Mist on the water, and the sun has yet to chase the chill from the air.

A barn, and a drying shack, I seem to remember. That's the light that paints the swan, paints the mist. That's the fire. The stench of fish, so, probably. I've never spent much time on this beach, not really. But this family's home is in flames, or at least I think it belongs to the woman whose screams stopped only moments before. Moments or hours, it's difficult to keep track. It's like I'm waking up, but of course I've been awake for hours.

Hours and hours.

The toe of my boot makes little boat-prints in the sand. The smoke from the shack stings my eyes, as the soot has stained the mouths of many here, black smears around lips and noses, flecked with spittle and blood.

The rowers pulled the staves from the goat pen and made a sort of cage for us, a meandering arc like half a ship open to the tide. There is nowhere to go – even if the three hundred of us were to run into the sea we'd be visible from all sides of the bay, and an easy target for stones or archers. And then there is the chill of the bay itself, of course. Mostly children and grandmothers left, and not so many of us strong for swimming.

We could turn and overrun the goat-pen. But they have thirty men ashore with shields and axes, some still blood-drunk from the night's work. Each of them could cleave a dozen of us before we reached the trees, and then they'd run out of people to kill.

Even if we made it, where to go? There are another hundred men sorting through what's left of the village. Little silver, if any, so that means grain and meat, some wire and iron. Nothing worth dying for. So even if I pushed past this small crowd, sick and lowing with grief, through the shore-hammered rank of posts, and somehow made it through the men who reek of smoke, and sweat, and blood, when they stand close and if some weapon found my hand, how many of them could I kill before the trees and then? And then? Then home, in flames or perhaps just ash and smoke now, it's been hours, and only more killing, them or me or both. But I don't move.

I hold my sisters close. Kara, exhausted, has stopped crying. Her fingers seem tiny when she reaches out to play with my hair, not as blonde as hers, but still blonde as ashwood. Rota hasn't cried, but she's shaking with anger. Rota would have killed three or four of these rowers before dying, I think, but she stays with us, to protect us. That's her.

We were taught, all of us, to pray in such hours. To swear vengeance or keen for those who now trudge whatever road to the doors of Valhalla. But I see little of this. We're still too bruised, too numb.

I'm thirsty.

We shuffle away from the rising tide, flotsam pushing us against the staves. It makes the men nervous, and their grip chokes up on their axe handles in anticipation. But we aren't going to do anything. They won't kill us all.

The biggest treasure is not whatever they might find in the village—not the bronze bell, or the plows, and tools, or scant silver. It is ourselves. Those of us who survive the journey will do well at the slave-markets of Upsalla, or Birka.

It can't be the cruelest of lives, to be in thrall. You rise, you work, you feed, you sleep. I've never seen a slave mistreated. They're too expensive. There is no freedom, no, not for yourself or any children you might have. But that's not so different to village life. And everything can be taken from you, just as it has from me, in the hours before dawn. They'll make me a slave then.

But it would kill me to be separated from my sisters, so I think we would all rather die.

I'm not myself. I am not the temper every villager knew and feared since I could walk. I am a numb thing, a frozen thing, cowed and broken.

I'm looking at myself, scared and tangled and matted, the drying blood of others on my dress and my face, and somehow I'm laughing. Just laughing. I can't stop.

Kara's eyes are wide. She's frightened of my laughter. But the thought of me as a slave is too ridiculous, and it's outweighing my self-pity.

Me, Ladda, a slave. I can't imagine it. Nor could anyone else. I used to bite people when I was small just for asking me to do anything, let alone ordering me around.

So I'm laughing and Kara shushes me. She's afraid, afraid that the men will come closer or take me from her or notice me at a time she desperately, so desperately, wishes to be invisible.

"You!" he says, one of the rowers who has penned us, herded us against the ice of the tide. "You'll laugh through a hole in your throat if you can't shut your mouth."

"I already have more than one hole to laugh at you with," I snort. The folk around me cringe as though bitten. The rower comes closer.

"I'll fill your holes with my axe," he says. It's a game now, but he doesn't know it.

"I think your axe is too small to fill any hole," I say, and the older women snicker despite themselves.

"Come here," he commands. I laugh again, though by now Rota has put her thick arms around Kara and drawn her backwards into the crowd of aunts and grandfathers.

"This is my beach," I tell him. "My land. Mine. You don't command me. You're no Jarl, and no husband, and no mother." I don't move. Honestly, I have nothing to lose by taunting him.

Nothing but my life.

"If you come closer, I will drown you in this very bay," I say, which is either challenge or invitation.

He doesn't know what to do.

"Look. That was an offer," I say. "You come over here and I'll drown you, and you can go bathed to your gods. It might take some time to get the fish stink out of you..."

"Bitch!" he barks. This just makes me laugh louder, and others are joining in. It's crazy. I'm getting us all killed. What in the name of Hel am I doing?

"That is a thing boys say to women when they are afraid," I say. "Don't be afraid, little boy. Come here and let me bathe you. Or are you going to threaten me with your... little... axe?" I illustrate this insult by lifting my little finger and wiggling it in the cool salt air. The aunts all laugh out loud now.

Enraged, he turns himself sideways to wriggle through a space in the posts, but he snags himself on his belt. I dip to the shore and take a handful of sand in one and a rock in the other.

He's free now and five, four, three paces from me, so I throw the sand into his eyes and the rock to his forehead. One of the aunts sticks out a foot, and he's on his knees on the beach.

I step back because I don't need to see what's happening to him, as the lame uncles and little boys, the aunts and grandmothers of the village, all grab whatever they can of the man and pull, pull hard, until he is torn open by their fury and their retribution, until he's a picture of the wounds we all bear now, drawn in flesh and spray and jutting bone.

Some of us have started to die. The other rowers have seen this havoc and have thrown axes and stabbed spears into the pen. Some are stupid enough to join their comrade, though those are soon dragged to their deaths, even though five, eight, a dozen of ours die to one of theirs. Each stone thrown from the pen is a spear tip thrust into it, until we settle and drag our dead closer to the water, though we can't say why. We have been, for a brief moment, agents of our own death, and that is enough of a life for some.

I would pray to Skathi, or Vor as my mother would want me to do. But it is still not the time for prayer.

One of theirs jerks like a puppet. Mouth thrown open, hands wide, head snapped back. A story-teller conveying surprise, though awkwardly. Comically. And his companion too: jerked back, shoulder-bitten.

Maybe someone in the pen has been praying. Maybe I should have been doing the same.

Then a third rower struck, though in falling we see the arrows jutting out of him, and the rowers turn and scan the beach.

I don't remember picking up this axe. It's curious. I remember my first comb, the first fish I ever speared. I remember deciding to run away from home when I was very small, planning the night before what bread I should take with me and a small pot of honey. I remember the face of the first drowned man I ever found, and the second. But how the axe came to my hand I can't say, and if you told me the goddess herself had put it there, I couldn't argue with you.

It's a small axe, the head the width of my palm, the handle alder. A throwing axe.

So I throw it and it finds the back of the skull of one of the Swedish rowers, the shock of his death reverberating through the air and back into my hand like I never let go.

The rowers turn now and run to the tree line above the beach. I'm stupid for a moment and simply stand there thinking about the man I've just killed. Two men, I suppose. One with my tongue, the other with that axe. I walk forward slowly to retrieve it when I see the posts are gone, trampled into sand, and the villagers tear after the fleeing men before they can escape.

More are coming. More men. A ship's worth of shields, maybe two. Yes, a full crew of eighty men and women, and whatever sunlight makes it through the mist glances off spear tips and axes and even a sword.

I think they've come to cut us down.

But among the men there are archers, and they let loose a volley into the backs of the retreating rowers. None make it to the forest, each with a thigh- or a shoulder-full of shaft and fletching and screams.

As the last of them falls, the eighty descend on them in a roar. Shields are driven into spines and skulls of our captors. The beach is a crunch and a howling.

Something moves past me, solid and fast as a boar. Though it misses me, the air around it shakes, slammed like a door. The fallen man, his back in the sand and now without his spear, looks at me with panic.

"Kill me," I say.

He looks for his friends dying on the beach, and back to me, not understanding.

"Well?" I challenge. "You have arrows in your leg. Pull one of them out and kill me with it."

He almost does it. He grips a shaft and winces, but that's all I need, and I fall on him, both hands on the axe handle, with all my weight, all my fifteen years of village life uprooted and lifted and hurled to the earth on the blade of an axe-head, crushing sternum and ribs and heart and ribs again.

The studs of his leather shirt bite through my dress into my knees. It hurts. My throat hurts, too, from thirst I think, but no, it's because I've been screaming, roaring, growling into the face of this dead man, this corpse whose shirt is hurting my knees through my dress, which I'll have to wash in the sea, or dye, because I've emptied him of blood and it clings to the wool and how long has this howl been in my throat?

Rota's arm wraps around my waist and lifts me up like I'm a doll. Even though she's fourteen, a year younger, she's stronger than me, stronger than anyone. There's an axe over her shoulder, sticky with blood.

"Come, sister," she says. "Ladda, come on."

I nod, looking back towards the water, catching a glimpse, over Rota's shoulder, of a single white swan.

"Take me to their camp," I ask Rota, still outside myself. The ones who killed the rowers, I mean.

"They're not setting camp," she answers. "They're going to follow them North, to Nidaros in the Trondelag."

"How do you know?" My voice is still hoarse, and I'm combing blood and sand out of my hair with my fingers.

"I heard them talking," she says. "Made sense to listen."

I nod. "I should go back. To the village."

"No," Rota answers again. "There's nothing." And she places in my palm a disk in silver, cold and hard, folding my fingers over it. A brooch. Our mother's. I can tell without looking. I search her eyes.

She shakes her head. The slightest of movements. So.

"Where's their chieftain?" How long was I on the beach? I look to the trees for shadows, but the fog has barely lifted and there's no telling the hour. A day without hours. Fitting.

Rota nods a direction, and I stumble following her. I take her hand, and it's only then I see she's cut her hair. Ragged, the line. Hurriedly, with a knife. Her hair is sometimes brown, sometimes copper in the light. I would braid it for hours when we were young, but I've stopped years ago. There are only Kara's birch-white locks to braid now.

"Kara," I say, remembering.

"She's... alright," Rota says. "She's safe. Come on. We should hurry, they're getting ready to leave."

Three men, in a circle of men. One tall and broad, with a youth's scruff of beard on the end of his chin like a goat, his hair pulled back in a knot. He stands easy, like he's waiting for fish or peeling an apple. Like war was nothing.

The other older, but not by much, and clearly wealthy by his tunic and collar. The third an advisor, with sun-bronzed skin and kind eyes, a step behind his wealthy master. The men around them part to make room for us, Rota and me.

"I killed a wolf once," calls out the bearded youth to me. "It was watching a squirrel up a tree. So I speared the wolf. Today, you were our squirrel."

"You were watching?" I ask.

"Waiting," he says. "We've been following these ships for three days. They must have thought us farther behind..."

"I'm no squirrel," I tell him.

The bronze-skinned advisor steps forward, smiling faintly. His eyes are brown. "This is your King, Ragnar, King of the Vestfold and of Jutland."

I pause. He doesn't look like a king. He is very tall, but his clothes are rough, and his breeches are unshorn goatskin so the sand and salt cling to the hairs lashed to his legs with leather thong. He looks half-animal at best.

"King," I say.

I reach up towards him and slap his face as hard as I can, my mother's brooch digging into my palm in my other hand as it makes an involuntary fist. There is a roar of laughter, as Ragnar dramatically staggers, rubbing his face for comic effect, mocking me. I have every right to expect a spear in my ribs now, but I don't care.

"King?" I yell. "You bring war to my village and I'm supposed to welcome you like a king? Where were you at dawn? We're all dead, save for the grandmothers and children! Some king." I spit at his feet. My hand hurts.

He considers this. He looks to one of his men and points, accepts something from him.

"For you, then, not-a-squirrel. Take it."

He hands me a sword without a scabbard. I take it, and it's lighter than I expect it to be. There are runes set into the blade, but I can't make them out,. I'm too exhausted and too angry and too thirsty to read.

"I can't feed my people with this," I tell him.

"That's no ordinary blade," he says carefully. "It's worth the price of a kingdom."

I thrust the sword's handle back toward him. "So sell me one."

He doesn't accept it, but he smiles, and not unkindly.

"You can't stay here," Ragnar says. "They may wheel back to escape us, or Fro may send for more ships."

"Fro?" I've never heard the name.

"King of Uppsala," says the counsellor. "His armies have killed your people and your king, Sivard. Ragnar has come to avenge him." I haven't heard any of this. Not a rumour.

"Do you have somewhere to go?" asks Ragnar. "Kaupang?"

"Kaupang?" I ask. "We are farmers. Fishers. We have no business in Kaupang. There's barely three hundred of us left. The market would swallow us whole."

"You would be safe," he replies.

"We wouldn't be anything," I answer. "No stories. No village. No names. We'd be undone."

"Somewhere else, then," says Ragnar's companion, the rich one. "Somewhere safe. Together."

"This man," says the advisor, "is Jarl Rorik, from Aalborg."

"A Jutlander," I say.

He nods. "Give me your name," he says. His voice is soft, the only softness I've seen in a lifetime, this new lifetime that began in the night.

"Hladgertha." I give him my proper name.

"I am sorry, Hladgertha," says the Jarl, "for what has happened to your people. And I would shelter them if I could. But Ragnar is right. It's not safe for you to remain here. You could go inland, or well north—but even then, the coast is not safe until Fro is dead."

"His head will hang from my boat," says Ragnar. But I've heard this before, men puffed up with the talk of war. All the boys with scruff-beards spoke like this all the time, until their lives were cut from them in the night. I try not to think of their bodies smouldering and cooling in the air, not a hundred famnr from this place.

"What boat?" I ask.

"We have a dozen skeid," Ragnar tells me. "You know boats?"

"My father... our father, is... was... a boatbuilder. Knarr, mostly. We sold them." I'm a thousand years old on this beach, I'm thinking. Remembering that other life, the life from last night, presses me into the sand.

"Do not set out in boats," warns Rorik. "Even if you have them." Which we don't—the rowers took everything seaworthy, towing them or setting them on fire—so it's a warning wasted.

"The Gaular," says Rota. "Our uncle has a lodge in the Gaular valley." I look at her, remembering. Summer's end, years ago. A journey, but not a deadly one. A run of salmon and my uncle's hall. A waterfall and a green forest soft with moss.

My uncle is here among the ashes of the dead. I don't think he'll mind.

Rorik looks to me. "The Gaular, then," he says.

I nod, thinking. "It will take a day for us to round up the goats. Some sheep, cattle, whatever's left."

"In the morning, then," says Rorik. "But do not mourn your dead until you are safe. Tonight, they drink from Odinn's own cup." These are meant to be kind words, but they fall to the beach before they can reach me.

Again, I nod. I thank Skathi for Rota's strength when I realize my hand has been on her shoulder, steadying myself, my other hand clutching both the brooch and the sword handle.

I turn, forgetting the king for a moment, and turn back to him. Ragnar.

"Your breeches," I begin. "Why would a king from the Jutland wear goatskin?"

It's an odd question, but he laughs. A story he's used to telling. "To keep adders away," he says.

"But," I reply, "we don't have adders in this part of the Nordvegr."

His blue eyes sparkle. "Then the breeches must be working."

Brushing Kara's hair calms us both—maybe she's too calm. In shock. Far off, as though she sailed away from the slave-pen on the beach, and the tide has yet to bring her back. She's clean, impossibly clean in her yellow dress with the blue apron, large oval brooches in copper like the unblinking eyes of some weird creature.

We haven't put up a shelter, as the sun has warmed these stones a little, and the moss is soft. Rota approaches, solid, and strong. She's changed out of her dress and into breeches, and found a rust-coloured woolen cloak from somewhere. I force myself to not scan the thing for blood stains.

Rota brings us steaming broth in a bowl for sharing. I thank her for this, but Kara says nothing.

"Do we have a number?" I ask Rota. She's been on task, and I doubt a drop of this soup has touched her lips.

"Two hundred seventy," she tells me. "No one alive between sixteen and fifty."

I nod. What else is there to do? We're now two tribes divided by a lifetime, the too young and the too old.

"The men have called a Thing," she tells me. "Sunset."

"Sunset is too late," I say. "Decisions need to be made now."

"You need to address them, Ladda," Rota says. "Tell them what the king told you."

"Why would they listen to me?"

"They're saying the gods have chosen you. When you lured that rower to his death." She sounds excited about this, and it should sicken me. But it doesn't.

"I got so many of us killed," I say. "It was reckless."

"We were all dead anyway. Dead or in thrall, all of us. We'd be in iron collars now if not for you." She sees my discomfort at this. "It's what they're whispering," she says, "and I know it's true."

Kara's voice is small. "It is my fault," she says. I hand her the wooden bowl which she takes with numb fingers.

"How? Shush now," I tell her. "You didn't bring Fro's men to us. Ragnar did that. Or some working of war, anyway. Jarls and kings. But not you."

"I dreamt it. All of it," she says, as though reciting something. Stumbling to remember. "The killing. The dying. The pen. The beach." Finally, she looks at me, after hours of dreamlike distance. "You."

"Just a dream," I say.

Rota speaks up. "If the gods give you a dream, they should tell you what to do with it," she tells our little sister. "It's their fault."

"I should have said," she answers.

"And we would have done what?" I ask, trying to hide my frustration. "Post guards? Uproot the village? It's already on us, and no one is guarding. No one is even packing." I play with a string of dry grass, tying a knot to make a wish, though I forget to before the knot is complete. I let it fall.

"Some of the boys have gone to get the goats, bring the sheep in," says Rota. And yes, if we listen, we can hear the bleat of them getting closer, though we can't see them from where we sit. We can see smoke, though, and don't speak of it.

There's movement behind the stones to the south. For all of us, our hearts hammer blood into our fingers, our faces suddenly cold. An indrawn breath of panic, shared between the three of us.

Comically, a long snout emerges, grey and with loose tufts of fur, and a black button of a nose. A great elkhound, with no small amount of wolf in his ancestry, looking for its master.

"He's dead, shaggy one," I call out. "They're all dead. Seek your master in Valhalla."

His eyes seem to understand.

"I'm sorry," says Kara quietly, holding out her palm.

Tamely, the dog trots towards us, three sisters in the pale sun.

The Thing is underway in what's left of the large pen behind the ruins of the barn. There's still the sweet-sour stench of dung. I've never had reason to attend a Thing before, and why would I? My life before today was attending to children. Working the loom and mending nets. Spearing fish. Gossiping with friends.

They stop talking as I approach, with every eye on me. I search their looks for blame, and see only fatigue, and fear, and sorrow. They're all in winter cloaks scavenged from the ruins of huts, hunched over a fire as if there was snow on the ground instead of spring grass. It smells like old men in here. Out here, I guess, with most of the walls gone.

"I've spoken with Ragnar, the king," I say, as clearly as I can.

"We know of no Ragnar," says one of the uncles, though no blood of mine. "Siward is the king of the Vestfold."

"Siward is dead," I say. "By Fro, a king from the east. Siward's son, Ragnar, wages war to avenge him." I'm speaking formally, and it's like having a stone in my mouth. A smooth stone, but still.

There's a murmur among them, and I don't know how to read this or any other sign. I continue.

"Ragnar has told us to move the village away from the coast. Fro's men may return. They may be coming now. We must leave."

"Ladda," says another fellow, not unkindly. "We cannot leave. We must attend to the dead. Our fields are good here. There is fish. These are our homes. Now leave us, child, for there is much to discuss."

"*Bestefar*," I cut him off. "There is nothing to discuss. We are leaving. All of us. Together. And now."

They are not used to such a tone from a girl, but it has been an unusual day. What would be met with laughter or anger still simmers, a fluttering of insult too tired to find a voice.

"The king," I say, holding out my sword, "has given me this as a symbol of this order. And even if he didn't, it's common sense. We're leaving."

None have seen anything like the sword before, or if so, not for many years. Holding it now, it is a fine thing, beautiful and singular in purpose. In the light and for the first time, I make out the markings on the blade: +VLFBERHT+, though I don't know what it's supposed to mean.

"My mother's brother has a fishing lodge in the Gaular," I explain. "It is not far, or not too far. There's salmon and forest for clearing with honest timber. Still time to get a crop in the ground, but only if we're alive to plough it. And that means we leave at dawn."

There are sounds of consideration. I continue. "The boys have brought the goats in. Some sheep, too, and cattle. We take only what we can't replace before the harvest."

"There is nothing, child, as you can see," says a third man, this one with a white beard and only one ear. "Only ash. And the dead."

"Pins," I answer. "Pots. Tools. Anything forged or wrought we can salvage. The rest we'll have to make do." This is too fresh a wound, the fact that we don't have a blacksmith. It takes the breath out of them. There's no fight and no objection, but there's no action in them either.

"We leave the dead," I continue, "and we remember them. But if we stay, we die, and then there is no one to remember them. The rowers could only kill them," I say, "but by staying—if we stay— we erase them."

They're ashamed, these men. I've gone too far.

"You have always had a temper, Hladgertha," comes a familiar voice. Brandr, a friend of my father's. He does not look at my face when he speaks, the shame of his own survival upon him. He should be among the dead, he thinks. I can tell.

"This isn't temper," I tell him. "This is... this is snow. Snow falls. You can take shelter, or you can freeze. But I tell you, the snow will fall. And we will leave for Gaular with the dawn."

There is a moment of silence.

"I will stay," says one.

"As will we," says another. "We must bury the dead, and say the words."

I tighten my grip on my sword. "Then you'll starve. At dawn my sisters are leaving for Gaular. And we'll leave you without a pick or wagon or cloak-pin."

"How dare you?" says the first of the remaining, more hurt than angry. "You do not speak to your elders so, child."

I'm angry now, exhausted from rolling this rock in the mud. "How many times must you face death in a day, *Onkel*? You were spared at dawn, unlike the others. You were spared on the beach. And now I'm trying to spare you from the rower's return or from starvation. You go to your gods a ready man, or a thinner one."

I sigh, the weight of the day upon me.

"Come to the Gaular," I say, turning from them. "I have no desire to forget any of you."

Forty-six stay behind, Rota tells me. I count them among the dead. Two hundred and twenty-four of us head east, keeping the Dalfjord on our right.

Before dawn, and with only a single candle, Rota and I picked out fragments of our old life. Pins. Pots.

Clasps. Anything quick, and light, that survived the fire. Wool and flax can be spun later. Hinges and locks, fire grates and tripods, these have been hauled to wagons. A snap underfoot reveals a bone comb, once beautiful, now trampled to shards.

The sun rises.

Everyone over six years carries a shield, if nothing else. Some of the shields are familiar stories, mothers and fathers. Others shields are alien and taken as a scrap of victory. But survival and memory are the only real victories open to us.

Before leaving, Kara disappears and again there's the hammering of panic in my fingers. But she returns from the forest's edge with a small bundle in wool, wrapped in twine. She shakes her head. "A secret," she says.

"No secrets," I insist. "Not today. Tell me."

Kara looks around for others, something she usually doesn't need to do. She's always just... known things. Now, she's being extra cautious.

"Alright. Come on." And she takes my hand into the forest, off the path into bracken that seems like nothing has passed there, not a deer or vole and certainly not a girl. But as she steps sideways, I can see it' is its own path, slender and wandering, into the stone of the hillside.

There's a little crack there, in the stone. Lichen grows on little shelves in the rock, and spider-webs still hold the dew. Kara turns to me, a finger on her lips, and slips into the cave.

Not a cave, more of a chimney. Like some giant bore an untidy hole from above. There is barely enough room for the two of us to stand, but light comes in from above and some from the narrow entrance.

"This is our mother's place," Kara says. "She always said it's the voice of our grandmother."

I'm hurt, just as I'm in awe. "How didn't I know this? Why didn't she ever tell me? Why didn't you ever tell me?"

"She was waiting until you saw her," she says. I'm confused. "And I saw her when I was very small. So, she asked me not to tell."

"Who's 'her?'" I don't think my head can take too much more of how little I know of things.

"Mama said that her uncle was the *skald* of her people, but when he was killed our grandmother kept his stories, and kept these, because there was no one else to keep them."

"These?"

Her pale hand reaches out and touches the walls of this secret space. And that's when I see them.

Runes.

Each letter a name, a sound, a story.

But I've seen runes before. I can read, of course, but there's a whole game to them I don't know. Even then, every spindle and pot has them, a little mark of who made this or that thing or who it belonged to.

"They're just runes," I say.

"Different," Kara says. "These runes are older, and closer to Odinn, who gave them to our mother's people."

"We're our mother's people," I say. Meaning all of us. The village.

She shakes her head. "From before." And she means the stories that are our grandmother's roots which stretch north and east, to the Finnmark, or perhaps even farther. Stranger.

"Show me," I tell her. "We're leaving this place, so we'll have to take them with us."

Kara smiles and taps her head. They're in there.

"No," I say. "Seriously. Show me. This is too important to lose."

My sister is still smiling, her strange, broad smile on such a tiny, narrow face. She takes my hand and places it flat against the cool stone wall. Beneath it, carved, is a stick with two shorter staves reaching out, like tree limbs, or like a figure offering something to the sky.

"*Fee,*" she begins, "wealth, and trade."

In the forest. It's so loud. The clanking of metal and the bleat of goats. Wheels digging ruts, the creak of ropes, and the whole village moving east and inland. Most of the hen cages were smashed to tinder, so we have the chickens on leashes of braided leather. It's funny to see them like this.

And suddenly, with the breath out of me, I understand Lars is dead.

Lars who, when I was a girl, I would watch herd the chickens to their pens, Lars whose laugh was the first to put a stone in my chest. The first hands I ever dreamt of. And now those hands touch only the cold earth, the same earth that nests my mother, my father. But their deaths haven't caught up to me yet, as Lars' does now. Perhaps their passing is waiting for me, each mil another name, or face, waiting to tug the air from my lungs and place a pang in my heart.

A mil. The length a man can walk his fields in two hours, or an hour's rowing. We are lucky to make two in a day, this caravan of children and *ammas*, of old men who have shed their walking sticks for spears. The children cry or sleep on the wagons, and sometimes they drag their shields in the dirt or trip over them, while the men let murmured prayers escape from white beards.

We rack the spears in the wagons, to form short fences on the sides. The youngest and the oldest rest their backs against them, while the cattle drag us through the narrow forest path. Mercifully, there is plentiful water rushing down to the fjord, and rabbits that some of the quicker children have caught.

All of two horses have been restored to us in the night, having bolted in battle and returning to find their kin taken in ships, just as we were meant to. For some reason, the elders keep asking me to ride, though I don't want to. We need to save the horses for the lame, so I walk with my sisters.

"We should walk along the cliffs," offers one of the uncles. "We'll make better time."

"We have shelter from the wind here," answers Rota, "and we'd be spotted by any rowers coming up the fjord. If they're coming back for us, I'd rather not give them our exact pace." Rota turns to me as she says this, and I nod. I love that I have to explain nothing to her.

Kara follows a cart, to which she has pinned some weaving. A belt, or trim. A chase of serpents in white and red. I wonder if this is the bundle she rescued from her hiding place at the edge of the village? But no, this is domestic enough, and no sense in hiding it. I can tell each loop and knot is perfect, like she was doing this beside a bright fire and not trudging behind a cart in near-twilight. The Norns, the witch-goddesses who weave *orleg* into our lives, are not as nimble-fingered. Kara is magic.

We stop and make camp. At least there's fire and pots of steaming water, rabbits and whatever bread or cheese our caravan has scrounged from our former lives being put to use.

The burden of the day shows in our shoulders. Stooped low and sloped to the ground, like boulders after generations of rain. Worn away.

Kara has a fire, and I make out the brightness of her quiet voice. Around her are some of the children who are not yet asleep in the cloaks of the *tanter*, the tribe of grey-haired great-aunts.

"A world of ice," Kara says, shivering. "Niflheim, so cold it would make night feel like the sun itself. And the sun world, the fire world, Muspelheim." She grabs each idea in the air with her hands, and pulls them far apart. "And between them, nothing, just nothing. Nothing forever. Ginunngagap." The children are rapt.

"But slowly," says Kara, wiggling her fingers, "the ice world sends a tendril of frost into the Gap. Closer, every year closer to the warmth of Muspelheim. And drip, drip, drip does the frost begin to melt, falling drop by drop by drop into Ginunngagap. Where it starts to form a puddle of cold water." She shivers again. Some children gasp, some giggle. Other simply stare half asleep into the fire.

"And the puddle grows. So huge is the ice world, that it has much water to spare and drips into the puddle, so much so that it begins to form the shape of... a giant!" And her hands spread wide and her shadow looms as she presses closer to the fire.

"Ymir," says a little girl. Four, I think. I remember the faces of her parents. Alive only two nights ago.

"Ymir," nods Kala. "He was the first Jotun, the first giant. But the drip made other shapes, more giants, and a great cow to keep them fed." If this reminds the children of their own hunger, their faces don't show it.

"The cow was Audhumla, and she found a salt-rock jutting from the ice. And she licked it, and licked, and licked, and under the salt was a tuft of hair!" and Kara picks up her braid and lifts it above her head, the children mimicking her, thick fingers stretching whatever locks they have, baby-fine or matted with forest, up to the tops of trees. An offering.

"And under the hair was a head, and under the head the rest of a god. It was Buri, the first of the Aesir. And Buri had a son named Borr, husband to Bestla, and they were the parents of Odinn, and his brothers, Villi and Ve."

"Villi!" says one little boy in delight. His own name. Kara smiles at him.

"There was a war between the gods and the giants, and Odinn killed Ymir. So great was his death that the other giants drowned in the blood!" The children's hands fly to their mouths at this.

"Yes, all the giants died, save two, who vanished into the mist, to Jotunheim, where they had many children to restore the race of giants. But Odinn took the body of Ymir, and from his body made the whole world. All the world. Not just the parts of it we can see, but all the world beyond that. His blood became the sea, full of salt. His bones and teeth the mountains and stones. His hair the trees," she says, half-whispering now, pointing to forest around us. "We can see the giant's skull in the dome of the sky, and his brains in the clouds. And from his huge bushy eyebrows," she adds, tracing her own, blonde, almost invisible, brows, "Odinn did circle our world, Midgard, a place for the first people, Embla and Ask, to keep out the giants, and the elves, light and dark."

On any other night, there would be a chorus of voices asking for more. A tale of the Aesir or the Vanir, of the war of the frost-giants, or of the elves, light and dark. But tonight, the children are bone-weary, rattled by the road that's little more than a deer-path. Too exhausted to grieve or even understand what we've had lost together. We're all of us a single bruise, raw and swollen and chafing under the weight of night and fading fires and the stones that are the teeth of a slain giant.

A keening in the night, and suddenly the air is so much colder. The children snap awake, eyes wide, gulping light out of the blackness between trees. The call again.

Wolves.

———— ◖●◗ ————

Some of the men, despite their age, have roused themselves and run to wagons, fetching spears. The *tanter* throw more fuel on the fires, piling them higher with what was set aside to be the morning's branches. We bundle the children towards them, the women in various stages of frailty or stoutness, but every one streaked with iron, and they grip shields in circles. There's no telling if this is a single wolf or a dozen, a dozen *famn's* distance or a *mil*. But wolves we know, an ancient enemy, who have culled children from these same families who now form shield-walls in the dark.

Wolves would avoid the village. But they know our caravan is a threat—each rabbit caught or deer felled for us is meat snatched from their pack, from their cubs. So they will cull us, plotting and hunting and dragging away the least of us, until we leave. And we cannot leave.

"Villi?" calls a voice from behind the shield-wall. "Villi?"

I look around for the boy from Kara's circle, but am met with each child's face searching one another's.

Movement. There, amongst the trees. A reflection in firelight?

Now it's my turn to move. Still gripping the shield, I make for the closest wagon and grab a spear. The weight is ridiculous, but its point ahead of me keeps me from crashing headlong into a tree. If I'm chasing a wolf, then I chase my own death. If chasing a boy, then I likely run only to join him in his own death. There's just no option. So I run.

"Ladda!" Rota's voice. A warning or encouragement, I don't know.

My breathing is already ragged, and my feet hot from blisters. I'm mostly blind, but there is a flash here, I think, or a sound just ahead, out of sight. A full minute, and no sign of boy or red eyes and bared fangs. A branch whips at my face, but I push through, until I'm no longer aware if I ran to save the boy or merely to escape the dead weight of infants and elderly, dragging them to some promise I made from the fragments of a half-remembered summer. I've lost all sense of direction, and could easily careen out of the trees and off a cliff. On, and farther on.

A sharp bark, there, to my right. But it's not a wolf: it's a child's cry of pain. Enough gaps in the branches and enough starlight that I see the fallen tree in time, and clear it in a leap toward the boy. Villi. His face a rune of panic.

"Villi, come. Come on." I drag him to me, my cloak around him, and he buries himself under my left arm, my spear arm. I scoot back so that I'm sitting on my heels, our backs against a tree and the spear planted at its root, so as to impale any wolf that might leap upon us in recklessness.

But a wolf is not a reckless thing.

When it approaches, it is calm. Confident. It's a monster, larger, I think, than a bear, though it couldn't be. Larger than a horse, perhaps, by some magic. Larger than me at any rate. I stare at its eyes to see if it looks for its friends, but if they're out there this one doesn't betray them.

There's a pain in my ribs. Two. One from the little boy, who's sharp chin is trying to hide in my skin, the other from my heart crashing like a storm against the walls of its house. In the half-light, the wolf's face narrows. Tenses.

It pauses, slacks, trots off a pace or two, the pads of its feet soft on the forest floor. Thinking? Toying? The reprieve passes, it's back and again its face a sharpness. A blade.

A blade with muscle behind it.

The wolf leaps and snaps in one movement. I unleash the great beam of the spear.

A white flash of pain. I've dislocated my damn shoulder.

All for nothing. I've missed, the wolf once again padding almost absent-mindedly. Sidestepping the fallen spear shaft which, momentarily, flaps on the ground like a fish. Alive, but futile. Impotent. Dying.

I draw the sword. I have been wearing it through two loops of thong on my belt, mostly because I had nowhere else to put it. I pull the shield closer to my body, resting the blade on the shield's circle, keeping Villi behind all of it. Between sword and shield there's a little window I can barely see out of, but it's enough because the wolf is inside that window, and all the world could fall away and there would be a girl with her back to a tree and a boy under her aching arm and a blade now heavy heavier still against the wood of shield that may as well be a hilltop under which to bury the both of us. And still, there is a wolf in the window.

My heels dig into the tree bark, raw in my shoes, but I'll not need them, neither shoes nor flesh in a moment, because this wolf is going to kill me. Kill both of us. There's nothing subtle about its intention now, its face a leer in the starlight. And then it owns the air between us, mid-flight.

Its body slammed by another, in the space between heartbeats, grey on grey, snarl on snarl.

Kara's elkhound.

The dog's size is no match for the wolf, which lands solidly and turns to face him. Cheeks slide back to reveal teeth forged for a single purpose.

I push with all I have left against the tree, hurl myself, meet the wolf's weight full against the shield. But my own weight is along the top rim, and the wolf pushes the wooden disk over, atop him like a lid, and we fall together to the ground. I am on top of a little round boat, the wolf pinned beneath me in a sea of snapping grey fur and ravenous anger. The shield protects the wolf as much as it protects me, while claws rake the ground for purchase. In a second, the wolf will right itself and those claws will kick me open like a fawn.

I don't mind. I'm too tired to mind. Too tired to really notice I've thrown the boy from me in my leap to my death, that he has risen and his hands are behind him, splayed out on the tree making the rune for protection, *yr*, out of some domestic habit or sudden insight into the way of the gods, I don't know. The dog barks and barks and barks.

But it's enough and the tip of my sword seeks out flank and snout, foreleg and shoulder, over and over, hitting earth more as not. And when the jaws come round the maw is larger than my head but the jaw is there and the blade slides along the linden wood finding fur and sinew. I push. I struggle to free my shield arm from the leather and with both hands on the sword's triangle of a pommel I push and try to climb onto the sword, pushing down and the scent is hot on me and I can smell the blood and I push and I push until there is silence save for my own raw and scratching breath. The dog's back is to my own, blood in its mouth, it's nose loud in the search for wolves. Maybe we didn't almost make it, maybe this wolf isn't almost dead. Maybe it's just a trap.

I'm not sure of the next ten minutes. Villi is crying silently on my arm while the sword cuts fur and hide in a familiar pattern, throat to tail, lightly so as not to gut the thing, along the legs, and after that it's just gripping and peeling and yanking away the stubbornness of it. Villi makes no sound, but won't let go of my arm. The dog keens constantly.

When the thing is done we walk back, the three of us, Villi holding my leg, the elkhound, and me. The wolf's coat is around my shoulders, its warm blood cooling against my skin as we stagger to the fires and asking faces.

A dream.

I'm in our house, or its charred skeleton. And my mother is there, cooking over the still smouldering beams. She asks me what's wrong, smiling, but her scalp is torn away, the blood there and the white bone beneath, torn like the body of Ymir making the world, making my life out her wounds.

I start myself awake.

Kara still asleep holding the elkhound. Or I think asleep. As I watch her, she opens her eyes and smiles a little. I note the fire has died out completely in the night, and my shoulder feels rent off and stitched back on.

"Your dog," I ask. "What's his name?"

Kara whispers. "He hasn't told me yet." She goes back to sleep.

I sit up as the caravan comes to life, perhaps an hour past dawn. Little boys pissing against a tree, others gathering wood, but no one ventures from the clearing alone, and the spears are no longer stacked in the wagons.

Brandr approaches. He, I think, is the youngest of the old, just as I am the oldest of the young. "Walk with me, Ladda," he says. I nod and rise, brushing moss and needles from my dress. He hands me a drinking bowl of steaming birch tea. I nod thanks, sipping carefully. Honey, somehow, the great-aunts again miraculous. I return the bowl to him.

"Where's Rota?" I ask.

"Gone. She went ahead at first light with some of the men to scout and hunt."

"Deer should be simpler away from all this noise," I say.

"How far?" Brandr asks. "To your uncle's fishing lodge? I don't recall him talking about it, but then I'm not sure I really knew him. Not well."

"I don't remember," I admit. "It's been years. I was eight or nine. This is the path though. The only path. We kept the water on our right until the ground meets the river, and the rocks become round. There's a great moss-covered stone, big as a house, and it's just left of there. North, I guess. Rota and I would run to the rock and swim."

"Is there a hall?"

"There's a house. Round, and large, or large to an eight year old. And a barn. Some sheds. We won't all fit inside. But we can build there, I'm sure of it."

We walk together for a moment in silence. There are cooking smells. He notices I'm limping a little.

"It's nothing," I tell him.

"You speared a wolf," Brandr says. "That is not nothing."

"I missed," I say, rubbing my shoulder. "Kara's hound distracted it, until I could get my shield on it."

"You're a very brave girl," says Brandr.

"No, not brave," I say. "Just tired. Frightened but too tired to care."

He almost laughs. "That is the secret of battle," he tells me. "But I'm glad of you, Ladda. You'll be the jarl of this new village. You know that, right?"

I stop dead.

"I'm no jarl," I say, confused. "I'm only fifteen. All I have is this dress, and these shoes will not last me the trip."

"It's your uncle's land, so it's yours now. You can be a barefoot jarl." He smiles. "The gods have chosen you. The morning on the beach, and last night with the wolf."

"Tell me which god has chosen me," I answer, "and I'll knock out its teeth."

"We will follow you, Ladda," Brandr says seriously. "To the Gaular, and after. Look well to yourself, and to your sisters. There will be much to do when we arrive."

"This winter will erase us," I said. "That's my fear. That we can't farm or fish or build with what we have left, with who we have left. And winter will find its way into our bones and our bellies and then we will be nothing. Will have been nothing."

Brandr reaches out and touches my hair, a grandfather's kindness, though I don't think there's blood between us.

"I do not think that is the fate the Norns have woven for Hladgertha." He thinks for a moment and rubs his belly. "And a winter with less pork and mead, well, I could stand to be a little skinnier anyway."

Without thinking I poke him in his belly playfully. To just be a child for an instant, it's a simple and treasured thing. He smiles.

But we have been made skittish creatures now, it seems. A single broken branch jars us from our moment, and we flinch at the sound.

One of the children catching rabbits, spear-staved grandfathers in tow?

No. A black shape, a tangle. Not an animal.

A girl.

Just not one of ours.

We talked about dangers on this journey. Of terrain, of wolves and bears, of wild dogs. Of the *landvaettir*, the nature-wights who slaughter livestock when displeased. But we haven't spoken of wolf's-heads.

Utlagi. Outcasts. Those no longer protected by law, whose life is as forfeit as the wolf who's hide Kara still sleeps on. Whatever crimes they have committed, which do not warrant death, receive banishment. No longer fully human. Most are scavengers on the outskirts of villages. But some become bandits on paths like this one, though there are no travellers here, so it wouldn't be much to live on.

Still, Brandr and I circle back to warn the others. We must be together—it's too easy for fading eyesight and the blur of boyhood to stumble into whatever trap might a bandit may have for hostages. How much would we pay for one of our own? More than we can spare, probably.

Dammit.

Again, the sound. She's close, this one.

I have an idea.

"*Meyla.*" I speak to the crunching bracken in the forest. "If you are hungry, come with us and eat. No harm will come to you."

Brandr simply stares at me. It's killing him not to speak, but he won't. I know this.

There is silence. I imagine her holding her breath, trying to swallow the beating of her heart. It's what I would do. I know the taste of this terror, the fear your very life will betray you.

"Meyla." *Little girl.* I try again.

"We are headed to my uncle's fishing lodge, in the Gaulardale. When we arrive there, I swear you will not be harmed. I will offer you again the protection of the law. If you want to join us, join us."

I am only guessing. I am guessing she is a wolf's-head, or the child of one. Perhaps she has never known a life among those who keep the law.

"You can come and eat with us," I say, "or you can go to your people and tell them about us. Tell them where we're headed. But we go to our own land, and we'll farm and build and fish there. If you help us, we will protect you. But if you mean us harm..."

I do not know how to finish this. But Brandr holds his silence, and when I look to him he merely shrugs.

"...we will eat you," I say, finally.

There is another dozen heartbeats of quiet, and then she bolts through the green like a deer, crushing the grass in a series of hisses.

After a moment, Brandr begins to laugh. A chuckle at first, but then a deep roaring, and I punch his arm to stop, but this he finds even funnier and he bellows laughter until tears come from his eyes.

"The barefoot jarl," he gasps for breath between howls. "Eater of wildling girls!"

I punch him again, but I'm smiling for the first time in days.

Hour by hour, the hills fall away down to the water, and the fjord becomes a river edged by forest. Here, finally, is the moss-covered stone, even bigger than I remembered. Rota looks to me, and we nod together, finding girlhood's path to our uncle's land. Our land.

We've exhausted whatever pity the rain had for us, a reminder that the gods owe us nothing. We're all soaked in minutes. I fear each cough is a grave, although whatever rest is in store for us lies not too far upriver.

At each stop, we count. We've lost only one so far, a *tippoldemor*, great-grandmother, and her missing likely not to a wolf or outlaw or illness, but to the forest itself. There, and gone. Half a day and better than a mil before anyone noticed the green had swallowed her. A turned ankle, perhaps, or just a surrender. I do not know what I would do, with all taken from me and so few summers to get anything back, anything at all. I ask this as much for myself as for the lost woman.

All night I rehearsed this plan, this pronouncement, one I must deliver with finality and without hesitation or question.

Rota has counted some twenty-eight households. I don't know if any of the buildings on the land are still standing, so I can't account for these. Whatever fields, fallow and overgrown as we may find them, will be held in common. That's the first rule. They won't like it, but I can't give them a choice.

I don't have any choices myself.

I'll get Brandr to pace out eighty famn in squares, and then each house will draw lots as to what to clear and where to build. They can haggle amongst themselves after that. There are to be common paths held alongside, and kept by the householders so there will always be a free path to the river and its salmon.

All past debts, all feuds forgiven and forbidden to speak of. What few tools we have will be in common like the fields, and those who lose or break them will repay from their harvest, whatever it may be.

The harvest will be thin, and the livestock kept for breeding. No slaughter this year. We'll forage, and fish, and perhaps any boats we build can return to the sea for seal in the autumn. This should see at least half of us through to next spring. Perhaps half.

There are a few law-speakers left among us, and I believe they'll see this as fair. Gods, I hope so.

It's smoke that greets us. A thin grey line against a thin grey sky.

I look to Kara and she smiles, and I don't know now if she's become simple from grief or if it's that her trust in the gods is greater than my own. But even in that smile is a certainty, yes, we're here on our uncle's land.

One fire. Not enough for a camp of rowers, then. The family of wolves-heads? The girl from yesterday? If they've kept up the land, we can grant them rights and a share, as is the law.

Kara's hound folds his ears back against his head, catches the smoke on the wind.

I know Brandr's eyes are on me, so I turn to him and nod. He hefts his spear, rolls his shoulders. Rota too is shield and spear, hunched forward, hips low to the ground and quickening pace. Stern, she peels away from the caravan and takes a deer trail to the left, to scout. The aunts hush the younger children, though one continues to cry in the rain, which will mask our rattle and wail somewhat. Still. They must know we are coming, have known for some time.

Nothing to do but what we have done. Trudge forward, a column of weariness in wet wool and thin leather, of hunger and loss and blisters. The wagons slow in the mud, each rock one more shock to the spines of the fragile within.

Rota returns in less than half an hour. She shakes her head. I know this means she has circled the land to one side and seen no movement. Inexhaustible, she takes a path to the right.

The road, such as it is, opens a little. I move my shield to my left arm and draw my sword from its loops on my belt, just to tell the gods I am ready.

I'm lying, but it can't be such a wicked thing to lie to the gods. They lie to us all the time.

Once-cleared land waist-high in bracken, with spring-berries beginning to show. Birds taking shelter from rain, so that a quick bow will see to supper tonight before they learn. Deer scat, so that, too, is comforting. Bear scat there, so that less so.

The land is a bowl, between a short rocky hill and a small fall off to a ditch that has diverted the river, a small dam upstream that has apparently withstood the seasons. There is the barn, its roof intact, and there the round hall, its roof not as fortunate.

Some of the men, despite their years, have formed a wall of shields, mostly out of tradition, and march to the barn. They'll fight for that first, if it comes to it. But it's obvious even from here that their battle will consist of chasing out spiders and rats, and the aunts are already organizing the children into tasks, fetching wood and preparing to sweep out. Some have begun picking berries as we pass them.

It's good.

The wagons, livestock, and drivers wheel to the barn, the smaller children in tow. The house-heads, Brandr, Kara, and myself, head for the hall. By the time we arrive, Rota stands at the open door, her spear's butt beside her ankle, its point at the sky.

We enter.

Someone has been living here. The scent of life, of food. Warm coals in the hearth, made here in the shape of a boat, not the long rectangular stone box of our old village. Rain spits in from where this arc of the roof has fallen, but it won't be too much work to restore it. New thresh for the dirt floor will have to wait, but we can use ferns in the meantime, and there will be sawdust soon enough with everything we have to build. The hall here, now that I take it in as a woman and not a child, is not much smaller than what we had there, by the sea. And fewer to fill it.

And that's the thing done. My task. I did it.

Some weeks away from sixteen full years, I brought the fraying remnants of my people here, and my life now is divided in two. A childhood there, by the sea, ending in death, and my life here, which begins under a sagging roof, and maybe death will leave us alone for a moon or two. Or more.

I should mourn, now. Weep for my mother and father. Weep for Lars who's the first boy I wanted to kiss, was going to kiss, was going to wake in his arms and smell his hair, but now there is nothing but the smell of wet earth and the cooling hearth. I'm still too numb, too tired, to grieve. Maybe my chance has passed.

Kara takes my hand, her braid white-blonde in the half-light, and I rise. There is a chair, the only chair, on the other side of the hearth, and she sets me there. Brandr comes around and lays his shield down, propped up against the chair's side.

And one of the *tanter*, a blood aunt of mine, or aunt's cousin at least, approaches sternly. Formally. She's carrying the wolf-skin, the same wolf I took with my fear and panic and anger and blade only two (was it two?) nights ago. She has scraped the hide, cleaned and cut it properly, laying it about my shoulders and pressing the brooch firmly into my chest. My mother's brooch. Kara nods.

"Jarl Hladgertha," says Brandr.

And I don't know what to say.

We've slept.

All of us, our tribe, either in the hall or the barn or in shelters in the field. We have slept and dreamt and snored, farted, cried, and turned in the night like one large, wounded animal.

Some kept watch, and those now sleep as we send out tentative feelers into the forest, upriver, along the ridge of the stone hill above the clearing.

I have declared my plan, for the lots. Some nod, resigned, others look steely-eyed to Brandr for his approval, those who find discomfort in accepting a girl as Jarl, even of such a modest household in which I find myself. A delicate moment. At least none look to the law-speakers for clarification. No one challenges me.

Yet.

There is some grumbling once the lots are called, and a small side market emerges for trades and easements and deals: a tree here, a path there. Goats or chickens trade hands, promises for future harvests made for various concessions. This is all fair enough and dull enough and I wish to the gods it was none of my concern, but of course now it is all that concerns me. I have led, and now must lead, mostly by sitting in the one chair in all the new village while all this takes place around me.

But then like the buzzing of insects, a disturbance or flurry outside. Heads raise from fingers drawing lines in the dirt floor, plans for barns, sheds, houses, paths. The children run in first, to herald her.

She is covered in blood, the old woman. The ancient woman. The dead woman. Alive and standing among us.

The great-grandmother lost to the forest on the journey. She drags herself along with a branch, stripped smooth and bound with leather scraps, the bones of small forest-things; birds, mice. One tattered crow wing laced to her walking staff by a thong.

The deer skin, newly sliced, still bleeds on her shoulders and forehead. She's pulled it over her head to shield her from the thin rain, which has only watered the blood down so her face is stained with it, every wrinkle.

None speak. None dare.

Who would? What is there to say? What words for this woman, pulled to the wild by her fate and restored to us so transformed?

"Hladgertha," she says to me, her eyes adjusting to the hall.

The others look to me, and I nod out of respect. I don't know her name, or I would answer with it.

"I will take the hilltop," she says. "Though nothing will grow there. Build me a house and I will keep it, for one twentieth a share of every house's crop."

Now eyes dart to each other, the numbers and fractions and values calculated instinctively. For each person here, that might mean an extra two hungry weeks each year.

"I will take three of the orphan children to be my eyes," she says, "and the bell from the old village. We will sound it for fire or rowers. I should see well north from there, and west to the forest, south to the river and the fjord."

An uncle clears his throat, or means to, and stops himself. The bell is our largest share of ready bronze, and some have it in mind for picks and ploughs. But these are things for warding off death slowly, whereas the great-grandmother proposes to ward it off quickly. And she most recently familiar with death, her advice seems well-heeded.

"*Tippoldemor*," I say respectfully mimicking the tone of a law-speaker, "the hilltop is not my land to give, but if you will keep it, then I will give you a twentieth of my share if nineteen join me, or a tenth if nine join me. I see the wisdom in your proposal."

Brandr places his hand on my shoulder in approval, though I wish he had not. I cannot be seen to be wanting it.

The crone grunts, turns, and trudges painfully from the hall. Each of us breaths more deeply, unaware that we have been holding back our lungs, out of instinct for those touched by the gods so.

The next day, and I ride.

Gods, to ride! Just to be myself, not the barefoot jarl but just Ladda, the boatbuilder's daughter, on a horse, alone. Everyone else seen to: Kara to her weaving and Rota to roam farther and farther from the village in search of threat. In the morning as Rota gets ready to leave, each time Kara's dog trots along beside her, and each time is sent back. Rota wants the dog with me, and here he is, horse-smart to keep his distance but still alongside.

The land is beautiful to me suddenly. It's a promise kept, and for the first time, I can see more than half of us alive a year from today. I breathe in all the way, the tide of my chest no longer catching on the jagged edges of my heart.

Here, there are straight trees I see with my father's eye and the boat-beams within them. The rain has gone, and the cool spring sun looks on the village taking shape.

Every tree smaller than the width of an arm has been cut down, stripped of branches and stacked. Stones dragged into lines and squares where walls will be. Homes. Little shrines on lot-corners or at the forest edge, here a stone with a hammer drawn in charcoal, or bind-runes of protection. A browning spatter of blood in offering. In thanks for our arrival here in the Gaulardale.

I should find a shrine to pray to. Skathi, Goddess of tide, probably can't hear me here so far from the sea. Var, then, as my mother's people did, protector of promises. Or Bragi, the Beautiful, who shines beauty on this place on this one spring day. I cluck at the horse, a dappled mare young and clever, and head for the hall.

Brandr is waiting, but I see his face mercifully has no news. He just waits for me.

"You should be building a house," I tell him.

"I thought you might need me," he says.

"Not yet," I say. "There are problems to solve, yes, but nothing I don't know about. Yet."

"One," he says. "The war."

"The war is far away," I say, handing him my reins as I dismount. "That was the whole point of moving here." Do I believe this when I say it? I'm starting to doubt it.

"A war like this, it's like a bell," Brandr says. "Once struck, it rings for a long time."

I brush the horse's nose, wishing I had some sweet grass to feed him. But I'm empty-handed.

"We've been pushed inland by the tide of war," I agree. "But I can't see us being dragged out with it. We don't have any warriors. We can barely defend ourselves. There's no profit in this war for us," I say finally. "We'll sit it out. Stay alive."

"Ladda," says Brandr. "There is much profit in war. And the gods have chosen you–"

I want to silence him, and he knows it. But he continues.

"No, it's true. I believe it. And this tide is upon us. So I believe that you will figure out a way for us to get in this war. And with it, the silver to build something here, something that will endure. So far, we've only been thinking of survival, but soon enough, we'll have to prosper here."

"We do need silver," I say, seeing where he is going with this, but not really believing my words. "We need a blacksmith. And it'll be years before we replace all the livestock. But how?"

"I don't know," he says after a moment. "I just know you'll find a way."

But then I do know.

I've always known, since that moment with Ragnar on the beach, speaking of skeith, and my father the boat-builder. And seeing the trees straight and tall on the land...

"Ladda," Brandr tries again, a different way. "What is it you want? Just tell us. Tell me, and I'll tell the others. We'll make it happen."

"If I ask this now, they'll resent me," I confess. "They'll want the year to build houses, clear the land, get a harvest in. Stock for winter. I can't ask them–"

"You can, though, Ladda," he says. "You can. Ask us."

"Ships, Brandr," I say. "I want us to build ships. That's how we go to war without leaving the village. That's how we bring in silver and tools. That's how we survive. That's our prosperity."

Each night the hall thins out by a dozen or so, as forest-shelters take shape into homes and hearths of their own.

I take my horn, the water cooling my lips as the fire is overwarm, and seek out Kara at her knot-perfect weaving.

"Tell me a story, Kara."

I've heard whatever she's going to say a hundred times, but in Kara's voice is the echo of our mother's. The legend is of my mother's people, from her great-grandmother's time or before, from the Finnmark, and that is as close to Alfheim as Midgard can get, so my mother was teased as a child for having elf-blood.

I know in my bones Kara has some elf in her. It's in her perfect hands braiding my hair. It's in her voice that sounds like a waterfall half-remembered. Even when she was a baby she was so still, so strange. Did she cry? She must have, but neither I nor Rota remember her doing it.

But this is why our mother gave her the runes first, because they spoke to her. And the runes kept her people alive, just as they will become part of our story here, and keep the rest of us alive.

"Ithunn," Kara begins, "was the most beautiful in Asgard, and flowers bloomed when she passed, and fruit ripened as she reached for it. So, the giants were jealous of her beauty and her growing."

Just the rhythm of story brings others from their tasks, children edge closer to the hearth.

"The giant Thiazi, who was Skathi's father, conspired to lure Ithunn away from Asgard, so that he could taste Ithunn's apples. For in each fruit was the power to remain young and beautiful forever."

She's speaking to the children now, her story rising with the words of giants, and falling into whisper with each mention of trickery or magic.

"So Thiazi asked Loki for help, and he, god of all trouble and mischief and cunning, did tell Ithunn of a garden, just outside the gates of Asgard, where the apples waited for her, and should she reach for them, their fruit would be the sweetest ever tasted.

"Ithunn left Asgard and sought the garden, but instead she found the giant Thiazi, who turned himself into a great eagle, and plucked up poor Ithunn, carrying her away to Jotunheim, and the hall of giants."

Old women clucked at this misfortune, and children gasped at the wonder and horror of it. The men found in it some humour of their own province, and whispered or chuckled.

"Without the apples of Ithunn, all in Asgard became weary, and then they grew old and grey." Her fingers make a beard, which wiggles, and reaches out to tickle the children in front.

"But it was Freya who knew that Ithunn's disappearance was due to trickery, and the source of all trickery was Loki. So Freya set about Loki, striking him even though she was now weak and old, and demanding from him the truth of what happened." Kara wields an invisible stick and is beating the children with it, who giggle.

"Oh, but Loki confesses to his crime. He said he had captured an ox and was cooking it, but no matter how hot the oven became, the meat would not cook. And when he looked to see what was happening, he saw a giant eagle, Thiazi, who had cast a magic upon it. Thiazi said Loki would always be hungry until he delivered Ithunn to the great eagle."

There was silence now. These children have known hunger, and the prospect of never relieving it. The men nod and sip from horns the last of the beer. Kara's elkhound twitches in his sleep, dreaming of rabbits.

"With Loki's admission, Freya gave him her magic cloak, transforming the god into a falcon, swift and dark." Her hands wings now. "And sent him to fetch Ithunn before the gods themselves would wither and die."

"And Loki flew from Asgard to Jotunheim, where he found Ithunn alone. With the magic of Freya's cloak, he turned her into a nut! And this nut he plucks in his falcon-talons, and flies as fast as he can back to Asgard.

"But oh, Thiazi has seen this falcon, and knows it steals something of value. So in his eagle form, the giant circles all of Jotunheim, looking for his captive. Never finding her. Finally, the giant understands. The falcon has taken Ithunn, and flies her home to her people. So the giant stretches his great eagle wings as wide as they will go, so they cover half the sky, and all the moon, and all the stars, and he drives the wind behind him, racing to Asgard.

"Loki dares to look behind at the roaring wind, to see the eagle bearing upon him. So he cries out to Asgard a warning. The great screech of a falcon. All look up.

"Odinnn and Thor begin a great and terrible fire, holding fuel in a pile beside it. In the distance could they see two shapes, falcon and eagle, knowing Loki and Ithunn are pursued by Thiazi and his terrible anger.

"The gods pile the flames higher and higher, so that Loki must beat his falcon wings so fast to reach over them, and even then, he flies right through the fire so that his feathers are scorched. And the stink is terrible.

"Oh, but look, the eagle, Thiazi, now is the size of a mountain, and there is not enough sky for him to escape the fire. Thor throws the last of the driest branches on the pyre, and as the eagle flies through he is consumed by the flames, screaming in agony as the fire licks the flesh from his bones and crumbles them into ash."

The children clap. But no story should end with an ending, but with a beginning of another story.

"But, the Jotun Thiazi, he had a giant daughter, Skathi, she of shadow, and the tides. She was a great warrior, and hearing of her father's death at the hands of the gods did outfit herself with links of iron and the leather of a great ox, so that no spear could penetrate it. And Skathi took her spear and shield and marched alone against Asgard, against all the gods there.

"Odinnn saw the warrior-princess Skathi, and fell in love with her courage. He sought to appease her with all the gifts of Asgard, now restored to Spring with Ithunn's returning. Indeed, he promised to serve her as husband, and set the eyes of her father Thiazi into the sky as stars, so that his name would never be forgotten. And so Skathi agreed, and was giantess no more, but goddess in Asgard.

"And now you must go to bed," says Kara, which is how our mother would end every story.

I make a face, a twinge of pain–not even pain, really, just discomfort.

"What's wrong, Ladda?" Kara whispers to me as the children are plucked away from the hearth by the aunts.

"The moon is on me, that's all, sister," I say. I will not dig beneath my dress but I know it is true. I sigh because there is much to do, and the men will not speak to me while I am bleeding. Much village business will have to wait, or fall to Brandr, and I fear of asking too much of him. Or having the others see him as Jarl, perhaps, I don't know.

"I don't bleed," says Rota, gruffly. I didn't know she was behind me.

"What do you mean?" I ask. "Ever?"

"Like a woman," she says. "I asked Gudrun."

"Gudrun?"

"The great-grandmother who took the hilltop, with the orphan children. I went and asked her my fate, and she knew that I don't bleed with the moon. She said I never would."

"You're only fourteen," I reassure her. "It might happen."

"It won't," Rota insists. "Gudrun told me."

"I'm sorry," I tell her, thought I don't know why. At the moment to be free of this burden seems a fantastic thing.

"No, don't be," says Rota. "She says that I am no woman, that I am to take a wife and die in battle."

I look to see Kara's reaction, if she will laugh. But she calmly accepts this news.

"This is some dealing of the gods?" I ask.

"It's my fate, Gudrun says. My *orleg.*"

"You're not… shaped like that. Like a man, I mean. I don't understand."

"She says that when I'm slain it is a man's ghost that will enter Valhalla," says Rota.

"And you're happy with this," I ask. I hope.

"I'm happy," Rota says. "Be a man. Take a wife. Find my life in battle."

Kara nods silently. My belly sends me another pang, as though to intrude on our conversation.

"Then I'm happy for you, Rota," I say.

"The god Loki turned into a mare and bore foals," adds Kara. "So surely the gods have chosen to make this of you. I love you, Rota."

Rota takes each of our hands and squeezes them.

"I have to find myself some moss." I hate to break up this moment, but the blood won't wait. "And Kara? Could you make me some birch tea? But Rota, despite your warrior's fate, please give us a year before you go off to prove yourself. Set it aside for a harvest and a winter. You're the only warrior we have, and I'd keep you here as our guardian. Please tell me you agree to this."

"I promise," says Rota. "A harvest and a winter."

A dream of a young man on a beach. I don't recognize him at first, but it's him, the brown-eyed boy between the scraggly blonde youth of a king and the and the kindly Jarl Rorik. Do I remember or imagine his golden skin, the brown of his eyes?

And there's the familiar sound of the village bell. Though faster now than in memory.

I am no longer dreaming, but the bell still sounds.

Gudrun, on the hilltop with the orphan children, somehow hoisted the thing into a tree and banging it as though Ragnarok were upon us.

Men are coming.

Too early in the year–and too wet –for fire. It must be men.

Rowers.

Rota' is already up, shield at shoulder and spear in hand, low to the ground and padding out the door, Kara's elkhound behind.

Kara herself isn't roused by the clamour, so I shake her shoulder. She squeaks like a kitten.

"Kara, wake up. Wake up. Go down to the river and hide there. Don't come out. Don't come out for anything. Now go." She wakes and smiles sleepily, moving and packing effortlessly but efficiently.

Even just propped up on one arm, my belly protests. My blood cloths are sticky from the night, and I'm both hungry and nauseous. I rise and arm myself with belt and sword, the wolf skin shaken out, cloaked and pinned to my shoulders. My hand rises to brush my hair but I remember Kara braiding it in my sleep into two tight rows alongside my head, and I awake with hair more perfect than if I'd spent an hour on it. Kara's elf-magic.

This time we will not be cowed. We will not be herded into pens for slavers. They've taken too much from us–even our fear. Now, they'll find nothing but anger and blood. That they would try to take again what little we've built here... I remember the crunch of bone beneath my axe, and find myself hungry for the sound.

To Hel with them.

Brandr is at the door, standing with the reins of the dapple in his hand. I mount the horse and ride, ride clear past Rota and the hound, north up the forest path to the right of the hill and the still-clanging bell.

Men, indeed men, but not on their way to war. Two boats-worth of men, a few women too, laughing, some of them.

Shields, yes, but at their side, spears slack and almost blithe at these angles. At their head, a youth on horseback, a blonde scruff of a beard on his chin, his breeches tufted and matted.

Ragnar.

And behind him, the bronze skin and brown eyes of a dream I had not half an hour before. I wish I knew his name.

I pull my horse up. We both catch our breath and there's movement to our right, a blur past. Kara's hound, barking and snarling. He does not look to me, but takes the whole column as a threat. The dog flies like a bolt.

Then a spear shaft, and a yelp of pain that cracks the air between us. Ragnar, out of sport or instinct, has thrown a spear into the dog at thirty paces, stapling it into the ground and killing it instantly.

Not instantly. There is one more yelp, a keening, before this dog goes to his ancestors.

I'm horrified, and my stomach tightens even harder than the cramps I woke with.

I'll kill him. I swear I will take the point of the sword he gave me himself and I will drive it into the front of his stupid goat-pants. I clap my heels into the sides of my horse.

He sees me, smirks, drives his own horse towards me, near laughing. My sword is out and I don't know if he understands I mean to gut him like a fish.

But he moves on a horse in a way I've never seen, like the horse is swimming, and he sweeps around me so that I run past him, and pull up hard to the point where I'm almost thrown.

He's circling me now, the smirking blonde and his horse. He clucks at my own dapple to calm it.

"That was my sister's dog," I say.

"It looked serious," he replies. "Did you set him on me?"

"I didn't get the chance."

"But you would have?"

"I would have. I'd set a bear on you if I had one, Ragnar Goat Pants." I'm practically spitting the words.

"That's King Goat Pants," he says, smiling. "I am sorry about your sister's dog. And your imaginary bear, too. Because I'd kill that as well to see you."

"What?" I'm confused.

"Why do you think I came to the Gaular? To see you, Hladgertha."

"Jarl Hladgertha," I tell him. This fetches a broader smile from him, which makes me want to kill him all the more.

"Jarl Hladgertha, then. We should talk."

"I have nothing to say to you. You're an ill-omen. You bring nothing but death and suffering with you."

"Well today, today I bring more. Much more. Speak with me, Jarl Hladgertha," he says. "It will be worth your time, and that of your people."

Ladda the girl would not speak with him. Ladda the girl would run and find a rock and crack open his head at a dozen famnr. But Ladda the girl died, I think, that day on the beach. And now Ladda the jarl will sit with the king, and see what he has to say.

I miss the girl.

He has, as promised, brought more than suffering. I'll grant him that. The village is constantly cheering as each crate is opened, each cask pried loose. There is even music as instruments come to life. The scent of food, and spices salty and sharp in the woodsmoke.

Kara is unshaken by the news of her dog's death. I thought I would have to find her by the river, but she was in the hall waiting for me.

"He told me," she says when I tell her the dog is dead.

"Who did?"

"The hound. He told me he died." Kara is very calm.

"When?" I ask. I'm worried about her.

"When he died. Before you returned. He spoke to me. He said your king speared him."

"He's not my king," I say, insulted.

"He is," Kara says. "The hound told me that as well."

I love my little sister but I can't take much more of this elf and god and ghost-dog business. I see Brandr standing with some of the other grey-beards, warming themselves by a tripod, even though the day is hot and flush with spring. It's the end of Einmanuthur, the last month of winter, and at its end I'll be sixteen years old and see the dawn of my seventeenth summer.

Ragnar sits on a box, part of a small circle of warriors who are all speaking in serious tones. Some rise out of respect when I approach, which is an odd custom, or maybe they have somewhere else to be.

"Sit, Hladgertha, please," he says. He's chewing on a small piece of dried meat, and tears off a slice, offering. I decline the bite, but sit opposite.

"Ladda, if we're talking," I say, trying not to look at him. His eyes are too blue. It's unsettling.

"Ladda, then," he nods. "We followed Fro north, but he turned, and we lost him in fog. He's gone south now to his allies in Jutland. My home."

"What does any of this have to do with us?" I ask. Maybe I'm being rude. I guess I am, but I'm trying to make a point.

"Well, we've turned south as well now. For me to be king in more than name, I have to kill him. Our boats are ashore to the north, and we thought you must be here somewhere. So, I have come to visit."

"A visit." He makes less sense to me than does Kara. And at least Kara's runes have something to do with me.

"We brought you some things we thought you might need," Ragnar says.

"Such as?" I ask.

"Tools, iron. Weapons. Oh, and–" Still chewing, he beckons one of his crew, a slight woman but clearly strong, who brings over a box similar to the one he's sitting on. She drops it between us and walks back to her tasks without looking.

"And this," Ragnar says, cracking open the box with his broad hands. I can see white scars there in the sunlight.

He pulls out a fine woolen dress, the blue of lichen-flowers. The colour of his eyes, actually.

I should be, what, flattered? Only I'm suddenly aware that my own dress is stiff with mud and still blood-stained. That I haven't washed my face this morning, and that my cramps are getting worse.

He rises and comes around behind me, placing something around my neck. It sits awkwardly atop the wolf skin, but I crunch down my chin and lift it up to see it. a necklace of linked bronze plates, beautifully inscribed with animals and birds. A treasure of a thing.

"Why... why are you giving me this?" I ask.

"Ladda," he says, returning to his box. "I think you should marry me."

"Why should I do that?" This is impossible. This entire conversation is impossible.

"I should be seen with someone like you," he says, smiling.

"You might remember I tried to kill you this morning," I tell him.

"You were serious?" he says, actually surprised.

"Of course," I say.

"You should marry me, and I could teach you to fight. Then next time you try to kill me, I will know."

"That's a fair offer." I think we are making fun of each other now. One question: "Why me?"

"Because I like you, Ladda. How you took down that Swede. Did you think I give a sword like that to every girl I meet on the beach?"

"You might," I say. He laughs.

"I would be a very poor king, then. That blade is worth a kingdom."

"So you said. I was going to let the householders plough with it." He winces at this.

"Well, now you know what we are talking about. I will have Eindr talk to you."

"Eindr?" I ask.

"You met him. He is one of Rorik's men. He has eyes like acorns."

"Brown," I say, defending a man who's name I've known for two whole seconds.

"Brown. But shiny. He's good at talking. He'll talk you into marrying me." Standing, he sucks the last of the juice of the meat from his thumb. "But now, I have to go and speak to my crew." He gives me a smile, more boy than man in that smile, but more real than any exchange between us yet. His fingers reach out and touch my face, very gently and not unwelcome, before he turns away.

"You should," says Rota. "If you want to."

"Why should I want to? How can I want to?" I don't know where to begin. "What would it even mean?" In the hall, seated in what was once the lone chair (though others have now arrived, thanks to our guests), by the long boat-shaped hearth. I have more questions than I could have imagined existed.

"You would be queen," Rota says, simply. "Think of what that would do for them." One dirty finger waved to indicate the village, generally. "But they aren't the ones marrying him." A pause. "What does Kara say?"

"She says the gods must will it, but they won't talk to her about it."

"Why not?" Rota asks.

"Who knows?" I answer. "But she says the elves will tell her."

"And what do the elves have to say about it?"

"She doesn't know yet," I say. "Only that they'll tell her eventually. I can't keep Kara's gods and elves straight. Or dogs, for that matter."

"Dogs?"

"The dead elkhound. She says it told her Ragnar was 'my' king."

"There you go, then," says Rota, teasing. "You can't argue with a dead dog."

Eindr, of the brown eyes, enters the hall. Rota catches my expression and rises to leave, giving my shoulder a squeeze in passing.

"Jarl Hladgertha," he says, formally. He's dressed in some Frankish robe, white with gold brocade in a palm-wide strip down his chest. Of course, he speaks for a king, but he looks so out of place here in my uncle's hall, with the roof only half-rebuilt and packed earth for a floor. Out of respect, I think, for our guests, I have changed into the blue dress gifted to me, though I have forgotten the collar. The wolf skin over my shoulders and my mother's brooch will have to serve.

"It's Eindr, yes?" I say.

"Yes, Jarl Hladgertha. It is kind of you to remember."

"It's just Ladda, please. I do remember you, you know, from the beach, though I didn't have your name. Where is your friend, in the green?"

"Jarl Rorik. He pursues Fro's fleet south to the Danemark. His hall is in Aalborg."

"I don't know where that is, except Jutland somewhere," I confess. "I don't know where anything is."

"I can show you, if you like. I have maps."

"It all seems a forever away," I admit.

"Three days, two maybe, with the wind. A boat is a swift thing."

In my head, I'm a child again with my father's boats, so new and yellow with the scent of fresh-sawn timber on the fittings, the ropes coarse in my small hands. I'm a wild thing, roaring with the wind, my hair gold as the sun in my face and the taste of salt and yes, yes, a boat is a swift thing and my heart trembles to breaking at the loss of my father–

"Jarl Hladgertha? Ladda?"

"What? I'm sorry. Yes, I just... nevermind."

"Of course."

"So, Ragnar," I say, trying to return to the present.

"Indeed. He has asked me to speak with you."

"He said."

"Before we speak formally," Eindr pauses, "will you accept some advice?"

"Please. So far the only advice I have is from elves and a dead dog.

"You have more advisors than that, surely," he says.

"I do. Well, I have Brandr, but I know what he'd say. He'd tell me to give my troth to Ragnar in a heartbeat," I tell him.

"Is that bad advice?" Eindr asks.

"He just wants my belly full. He wants me fed and safe."

"Then no, it's not bad advice," he says, almost allowing himself a shrug. "However, I would offer this: marriage is business, and business is war. You win by knowing–truly knowing–what you set out to achieve, and then put in place all that is required to achieve it." He is being kind, but he's nervous. He thinks he's overstepped his role here. "So," he's half-whispering, "what is it you want?"

I think for a moment. It's embarrassing how long this moment is.

"I want us *all* to be fed and safe. Here. I want war well away from us. I want us to make it through the winter, though it is only spring, and the next winter, and the next. I want the story of my people to survive. I want my mother's… legacy to survive. That's what I want."

Eindr nods. He has much to say, but he's holding back.

"So we are going to build ships for the war," I continue. "Especially now we have tools and more hands to work them. And Ragnar can take our ships to war for a share, and that share will feed and secure the village."

Again Eindr nods. "A solid plan. But you need hands..."

"Ragnar's crew," I interrupt. "I want some of them to stay. To build, to plant. To make boats."

"Ragnar will want to bring his crew with him south, to the war," cautions Eindr.

"He has hundreds. Leave us two dozen."

"Two dozen warriors is a modest bride-price, Ladda."

"If we took more we'd need to feed more. We need strong backs and spears. There are wolves in these woods, on two legs and four."

"Understood," Eindr says. "But know that Ragnar has lands, and from those lands come taxes in silver and wool. Bronze too, and trade to the south and east."

"I don't understand those things, and you asked me what I want. Well, I want what I understand. I know we need parents for our orphans and a crop in the ground. I want Ragnar to buy our boats as we build them. And that way we survive, all of us."

And Kara's runes, I think. *My mother's runes, the secrets of her people. My people.*

"That way we don't disappear."

I wake in Ragnar's arms. I do like the scent of him.

I like too how the hall has been roomed off with thick woolen blankets, and our bed warmed by not one but two tripod fires kept going all night without having to wake to tend to them.

In the half light of dawn, I look at his sleeping skin. I look at the body of my betrothed.

He's lean. His shoulders are earned, not born, as the aunts say, which means he is not large by birth but by work. Were he a boat he'd not be a buss, with its broad beam and deep draught, or even a karr, narrower and sleeker, but a skeid—a thing light and nimble on the water.

He wears his hair in glibs. Shaved up the sides, and grown longer at the top, twisted into mats like pine cones. These are waxed, with some kind of fragrant oil he also uses in his beard. Even for a man who wears goat-pants, he's not completely without vanity.

I wonder if I ought to be in love. In some weeks Ragnar says Fro will be dead, and he will truly be king, and I shall take an oath before Var and him as husband. A queen, then. But love? I've come to admire Ragnar in these days. I was foolish to dismiss him so readily, but he says I don't need to apologize for my anger, which was warranted.

I like kissing him. I like waking up to him. He makes me laugh. And I think I trust him, a little, at least.

So we understand each other in this.

"Shield up!" Ragnar calls. His sword cracks again and again on the rim of my shield as I keep it high, duck my head nearly into my shoulder and lean into the boss, the metal hollow that protects the hand. There's nothing gentle in his blows.

"I thought we were practicing!" I shout over his assault. He withdraws, panting.

"We are practicing fighting, not practicing playing," Ragnar says.

"I've only seen training with branches," I complain.

"That will teach you to protect yourself from branches," he says in all seriousness. "How about we find Fro's army and ask them politely to use branches because we're not ready for swords?"

"If a sword is worth a kingdom, I'd imagine we'd see more branches," I say, brushing the sweat from my forehead.

"Not every sword is so valuable. Just that one, and its kind," Ragnar tells me.

"Why? I've been wondering that since you gave it to me."

"Let me see it," he says. I find myself reluctant to hand it over.

He props his shield at an angle against the base of a tree, kneeling before it.

"So," he says. "This is my enemy standing, yes? And this is me standing." He means the shoulders are at the same level. I nod, understanding. He takes a few thrusts around the shield.

"I am not attacking the shield, but the one behind it. But he is not so ready to be stabbed, so he blocks with the shield, over and over. Like so." And Ragnar changes his thrust at the last minute to stab at the shield itself to demonstrate.

"A sword is not an axe. It is not for chopping, and has no hook for pulling the shield down. Also, it is not a spear; it has no shaft and no shoulder behind it. So it must seek where the shield is not. And most times, if your enemy is good, it will fail to do so." Again and again, the sword thuds against the shield, harder each time, sending little flecks of linden wood into the air.

"So the sword itself must take its own blow, if your enemy's skull refuses to do it. See how it bends? With each strike, it bends and snaps back. It does not stay bent; it does not shatter."

"All right," I say.

"Most swords stay bent. Or shatter. Not the first time, or the tenth, but eventually. Which is why an axe is better, or a spear is better. Unless it is *this* sword. *That* is what these runes mean," he says, meaning the +VLFBEHRT+ letters set into the blade.

"So a sword that strikes a hundred times..." I begin.

"Is worth a hundred warriors, yes." And Ragnar and I again understand one another "And with a hundred warriors..."

"You can carve yourself a kingdom." He returns my sword to me. "I'll make you a sheath for that, to keep it out of the rain."

I turn the weapon in my hand, admiring once more its beauty and its balance. Its purpose.

"Pick up your shield," Ragnar says. "Again."

In the night my shoulder aches as I turn, and my elbow is a solid bruise. But I've learned to not simply hide behind a shield, but to use it, to move the force of an attack around me. To break a spear like a wave on a rock. To transform from a wall to a flat thing like a table that can be driven into throat or collar bone. And with the sword to take an axe-hand, or an ankle. Flexing my hand, I wince a little and wonder if I've broken my little finger.

I place my hand on Ragnar's chest, watch it rise and fall as he sleeps. Like the tide, the distant tide of my childhood, receding in the dark. Little Ladda, sailing away, never to return.

I don't know how much of this is routine discipline among the crew, or a show for the villagers. But it does set the grey-beards to roaring.

We form a shield wall on command. We step on command, spears resting on the shields to our right. We thrust on command, withdraw on command, step again, forward, back, on command.

A second row of warriors with longer spears, shafts as big as my forearm, send a chorus of spear-points over our heads. Then on command (always on command), we drop our spears by our sides, pull the axes from our belts, and swing in unison, each shield opening slightly but covering the warrior on our left, ourselves protected by the shield on our right. And repeat until the breath is ragged in the throat and the arms are burning.

As the smallest (though not the youngest, this falls to Rota), each step for me is a stutter, a step and a half. Voices behind me telling to me to raise my shield up, up, up higher, so that I can barely see over it. But if I dig my hips into the motion, I'm strong and solid on my feet. I have to resist the temptation to skitter to catch up with the others, slowing my movements so they are deliberate, focused.

There is a woman here, and she has decided she does not like me. Perhaps because Ragnar has chosen me, or I remind her of some past rival. There's no telling.

Still, we are pared often because she is not that much taller than me, but her blows are meant to kill with each axe-strike to my shield.

We circle one another in the wet earth, she with her spear clutched tight to her chest, the point barely a palm's width from her hand. I raise my sword to catch the thrust, and turn it, but her jab is a feint, and as my sword reaches out she spins the spear's blunt end to catch me square in the chest, winding me and knocking me into the dirt.

Gasping, I note two three things: the first, that I didn't drop my sword. The second, that I will always remember such a spear-grip, improbable for thrusting. Thirdly, that I bear no anger to my attacker, because she has taught me the first two things.

A hand reaches out to clasp my forearm and near-tosses me into the air like I'm nothing. I'm on my feet and looking into a dark red beard.

"Not bad," says red beard. "Keep your feet under you."

"I'm better at sea," I tell him, catching my breath.

"Oh, you're a pirate girl," he smiles, mocking me.

"My father was a boat builder. I had my sea-legs before I could walk on land."

"That'll be useful," he says gruffly. "Still, keep your feet under you."

Nodding thanks, I square off against my opponent.

Again.

Ragnar's crew of eighty strong backs do in a week what would have taken our two hundred a year. There is a new barn, pens hammered into the earth, gates with hinges. The hall is clean, the floor leveled and inch-deep with sawdust, the roof tight against rain and snow. Trees felled, and timber squared for building. An oven, a kiln, a forge, brambles cleared, and rows for planting. Fish sheds by the river. But that leaves hunting.

The deer will get smarter and farther afield. So that increases the likelihood of running into others, if there are others. Most likely upriver.

So, in the morning Ragnar and I will ride, just the two of us, until dusk, and return after nightfall, seeing what we can see. But before then, Brandr has a task for me.

At dusk he comes to me.

"There is to be a blooding tonight," he says. He leans on the spear he uses as a walking staff. He's tired. "We have no priests, so it falls to you."

"We should keep the cattle," I argue. "For labour or breeding. Slaughter them when winter comes, we'll need the meat."

"Without appeasing the gods, we'll not see the end of winter," he says, "and the salmon should be good this year."

"I do not think the gods talk to me, Brandr," I tell him. "I've waited and tried, they know. I went with my mother and made a shrine to Var in the forest, our old forest, but nothing ever happened."

"The gods may not speak to you," Brandr says, "but they listen. They are watching you, Ladda. And you should be seen to do this thing."

"Kara should do it," I say, seeing the obviousness of it. He ponders on this.

"She is not strong enough to kill an auroch with one blow," he says.

"Neither am I. But she can say the words, and one of Ragnar's crew can slaughter the bull. Or Ragnar himself can swing the axe, the people will like that."

"The gods will like it, I think, yes." Brandr nods.

I look for Kara to speak with her, but she's not in the lodge.

Movement there, up the path and into the woods. More of a fluttering of darkness, against the fading twilight.

She's not far along the path. She sits on a moss-covered rock, waiting for me. She tells me as much.

"What are you doing?" I ask her. She's become so strange, so distant, since all of this happened. I barely recognize her. Her face is the same, my little doll of a sister, her cleverness and quickness. But there's something else to her now, something I don't understand. She's been somewhere the rest of us haven't.

She doesn't answer, but looks down at her lap. And there is the bundle, the secret bundle, in blue leather wrapped in thong. The thong's since become a braid, and there's a bead there now of bone or stone I can't make out in the dark.

Unwrapping, I see it's a bundle of sticks. Staves, actually, the length of a hand, but each as narrow as her little finger. A single glyph carved and stained into the end of each one.

Runes.

"I've been speaking with them since we got here," she says. "That's how I've known."

"Known what?" I ask.

"Everything. About you and Ragnar. About the blooding tonight, and why you've come."

I rub her back, just taking all of this in.

"Do you see the dead?" I ask. I have to ask. "Have you seen our parents?"

She shakes her head. "Father is in Valhalla," she says. "He died protecting us, iron in his hands."

"And our mother?"

"She's somewhere else. I can't see her."

"Somewhere else? Where else is there to go, but Valhalla or Hel?" I'm desperate now. "Kara, is our mother with Hel?"

"No, silly. She's somewhere else. I just don't know where that is yet."

"Perhaps she's gone to Elfheim, where they say her people were from."

"I can't see into Elfheim, even with these," she says. "But I like to think so."

"I need your Elf-nature tonight, little sister," I say.

"You want me to preside over the blot," she answers. Nobody's told her, I'm sure of it. It's just one of the things she knows.

"Please," I ask her. "It just seems... right. You're better at this than I am. Things with the gods, I mean."

Kara looks at me and smiles, but it's a strange and disconcerting smile.

"You haven't seen her yet?" she asks. "No," she says, answering her own question. "Soon, though."

"Seen who?"

She picks up the rune staves just a palm-width above their leather shroud and drops them again, peering.

"You'll see," Kara says, pressing a stave into my palm.

Perth. The dice-cup. The vessel from which chance emerges.

There are different ways to do this, they argue. Almost always during the day. Only rarely at night, which means something different. They are debating what, exactly.

Still, fires are lit, and the great black bull, skinny as he is but still a mountain of a thing, comes along on his rope, either not sensing his fate or not caring.

Not sensing, it must be.

There's quiet, but when Kara appears in a long tunic of white flax I've never seen before, there is silence. The difference between quiet and silence is something I've never felt before, but it's on me, on all of us, like a weight now.

The words she speaks are in a language none of us know. None of us have heard it. And when she sings to the flames and the bull and the night, her chant is weird and terrifying and beautiful; a tune that opens the heart as it chills it, words that haunt the caves of our bones. A mist clings to her, and I notice the runes that form there, hardly believing I can really see them. *Othal* for land, heritage, and belonging, and *jera* for harvest, and the *berka* for new beginnings. The runes are things as much as song as shadow, and any surprise I feel is distant, dreamlike, chastising myself for not having seen them before. But I see them now and their simple ask; *let us belong here, give us a year, give us a spring. Please.*

And when her song stops, Ragnar's axe falls heavy on the beast's neck, and the animal crashes to the earth with a moan and a hot spray of blood that glints black in the firelight.

Brandr takes the broad bowl to catch the flood of gore, the scent thick in the night air, the metallic heat already catching in the back of my throat. With great solemnity, each of us dip a finger into the bull's blood and mark a spot special to each, for blessing: lips or eyelids, chest or belly. Rota streaks crimson along one forearm, catches my eye and nods, as she always does.

I suck the blood from my fingertip. I'm going to need the auroch's strength in my body. I need the blessing to fill the hollowness there, to ground me so I don't blow away in the next storm. The taste is copper on the tongue.

And when each has had their turn, the bowl is presented to Kara, and the look in Brandr's eyes is almost fear as he hands it to her arms, the weight of it obvious. She chants the names of gods I know: Thor and Odinn and Frey, Freya and Bragi and Baldr, Var and Skathi, but also others I've never heard of, elf-kings or giants perhaps. With effort, her slight arms raise the shallow bowl of now-cool blood and she tips the entire thing over her head, transforming herself from some kind of white flower in the firelight to a nightmare.

She paces, like a dance and like sleepwalking, through and past the circle of watchers, each bloodied now, and we fall in line behind her as she walks to the main field behind the lodge. Staves hammered into the ground and string marking rows to plow, or what to plant at which time as rain and the moon will allow.

Kara stops, like a pendant suspended from the sky, and we each of us come to a less elegant pause, stumbling a little in the torchlight and uneven ground. My sister, covered in blood, throws herself face first into the mud of the field, as though diving from a cliff. Then still face down, bloodied arms spread out in a rune.

Tyr. An arrow aimed at the sky.

For a moment I fear she's dead. That the gods have taken her from us because she's so perfect.

It is Eindr who reaches out to her after a painful silence. Takes her arm. Brushes the bloody mat of hair from her eyes.

Then she rises to one knee, no longer an elf-thing but my little sister, the same child I held in my arms when she was a baby, out of whose mouth I would pluck beads or stones or other things she'd find to choke on, whose back I'd rub in the night after troubled dreams. Just a girl.

She's just a girl. I keep telling myself that.

Ragnar wakes me at dawn, with a kiss on each of my eyelids, his fingers gentle on my cheek.

As the fur slides from my shoulders, the air is chill on my skin, so I make to pull it back up but he stops me.

"No, no time for sleeping," he says, kissing me again. "Now, we ride."

My horse has been readied for me, and the aunts have dressed me and wanted to re-braid my hair, but I tell them to leave it as Kara had set it, with smaller rows tight against my head, and the rest spilling down my back.

There's a polished silver plate, and never before have I seen myself so clearly. Sort of half-way between Kara's white-blonde and Rota's coppery brown, or perhaps blonder than that. My jaw, too, is softer and rounder than Kara's point and Rota's square. My lips are full, and I wasn't aware of this before.

In minutes, we're clear of the village and any sign of others. I can only guess that Ragnar has dismissed whatever bodyguards would insist on riding with us.

"It's good for the two of us to ride alone, in silence," he says.

"Why in silence?"

"So we can see if we're going to be friends," Ragnar says.

"We're not friends?" I ask.

"You have my troth," he says. "It means I'll care for you, no matter what. But it would be good if we were friends."

"Why?" I'm laughing at him.

"Because when I do something stupid, it'll be easier for you to forgive me."

"Are you planning on doing anything stupid?" The rhythm of the horses makes this kind of back-and-forth easier. He's been my lover for a week and only now is he flirting with me, or at least in any way I can recognize.

"Only someone wise can answer that. So, I have to say I don't know."

"And you're not wise, Ragnar?" I tease him.

"Oh no. You, I think, are wise. Me, I'm just stubborn."

"I can be pretty stubborn," I admit.

"I know," he says.

"You know?" I pretend to be insulted.

"I've asked," he explains. "You're famous for it. Ladda the stubborn. You are a legend. There is a great hall in your honour in Stubbornheim."

He has me laughing freely now. It feels good.

"So if I slay you in battle?"

"Oh yes, we will meet in Stubbornheim. In the great hall of Ladda the Stubborn."

"I think we should go back to the plan where we ride in silence."

"See? That is very wise, Ladda."

And we do, for hours, the horses following deer trails. We stop to pee or eat apples, and we have some salted fish he has brought from his boats. The sky is clear save for high thin clouds, and only the threat of spring rain well to the south.

The horses are too loud for deer or bear, though we see signs of passage for both. Nothing human though. While it is a bright and simple day, with only the faintest ache from riding, we are still both of us attentive, with each rustle of birds or squirrel chatter a possible warning. But there is nothing but the slow arc of the sun sliding into afternoon.

"We should go back," he says. "Before it gets too dark."

"We could go farther a few hours and just camp. I don't think it'll rain."

He stares up at the sky for some time.

"An hour then," he decides. "Then we go back."

I cluck the dapple ahead in agreement.

For almost an hour, nothing but the green of the day, the forest the same as the one since dawn.Only the light has changed. But my horse has caught the scent of something, and I hold him up.

"What is it?" I whisper to the horse.

But then I catch it too, and look to Ragnar, who sits tall and alert on horseback.

Smoke.

He beckons silence and slips from his horse. I do the same. We unstrap our shields and tether the horses together, though loosely, and we make our way down the trail calm as sticks on a current.

The path opens and the trail falls away somewhat, another bowl of land by the water similar to our own village, complete with the low hill to the north.

A much larger village. Here the river is closer, not dammed to a creek but the full river itself, so there is a dock and boats. I look at Ragnar and he is counting, counting men and counting horses, counting buildings and counting animals. He gestures we return.

When we get back to the horses, he says nothing, for fear that our voices might carry or that someone may have seen us, may be tracking us. For an hour I follow his horse, my mouth dry and my heart hammering. Because I know what it means.

It's a matter of time before this village discovers our own, before our hunters meet one another in pursuit of the same prey. A matter of time before we both want the same thing and there's not enough to share. Before they can mount a challenge we couldn't repel, even with my bride-price contingent of Ragnar's forces staying behind.

"My mind is racing, Ragnar," I tell him. "Stop, please. Talk to me."

"I know what you're thinking, Ladda," he says. "There are a few options."

"All right," I say.

"First," he pauses longer than he should. I'm anxious. "We could move the village. South, south of the fjord. Or east to Kaupaung."

"We would never survive the journey," I insist. "Not all together. And east would lead us right through that village, and through others."

"South, then. South to the sea, to my home in Jutland. Viborg, maybe."

"How?"

"You're already building boats. Build more and get in them."

"These people are not Jutlanders. This is our home," I plead.

"What would you have me do?" he asks. "What?"

"You are the king," I remind him. "Send word to that other village that we are under your protection."

"Ladda," he sighs. "I am king to who? To my ancestors? To my father? To the gods? Or just to my crew? No. I must kill Fro. Then everyone will know I'm king. But until then... they just see me as eighteen, spending a chest of his father's silver on a handful of boats."

And I had not seen until that moment how young he was. His scars and his fierceness, his muscle, yes, all these masked that my betrothed, my king, was so close to my own age.

"Besides," he says, "in a year my men will want to go home anyway."

"What do you mean, home? They are home. The Gaular is their home."

"Ladda, these men, they have fields and wives of their own. They stay because I pay them to stay. I can't pay them forever, and they wouldn't take my silver to stay."

"So a year? My bride-price buys me two dozen men for a year?"

"Yes. Did Eindr not explain this to you?" He's genuinely puzzled.

"No. Yes. He may have. I just thought..."

"They're not slaves, Ladda. They joined me for a share. For silver. And to stop Fro from raiding their homes in the south."

"Ragnar," I say calmly, though I am shaking. "I can't marry you if you can't protect my people."

"You'd break our troth?" He's hurt.

"Haven't you broken mine?" I'm trying to not yell. Trying not to cry. "You came to find me, you made an offer. I only accepted this because we needed your help."

"You had my help. We've built. We hunted. We repaired. You'll make it through a harvest and a winter. And if I can end this war, you can stay forever."

"So stay and fight, Ragnar," I plead.

"I go and fight, Ladda," he tries to explain. "For you, for them. For all of us. At month's end we return south and find Fro. I want you to come with us."

"Why? I won't marry you, so why will you have me?"

"Because," he says, turning his horse to me in the night. "Because we are friends."

At the boatyard, or what is to become one.

The sound is soothing. It's the sound of my childhood, of my father's hands, and the promise of adventure with each new boat as we would take her out for the first time. Chunk and scrape and the *zzif* of saws.

The familiar patterns taking shape, from keel and strake, overlap and beam, stringer and scarf, rib and knee and gunwale. All in gleaming new-sawn wood, and a treasure of rivets. This is a karr taking form here. A warship.

Ragnar's crew are wrestling *glima* on the shore, trying to grapple one another into the water. Each grip countered by a twist or escape, and this met with a trip, or a wrist lock. We've all known each move since we were children.

I could stay. I could remain with my people and simply work the boatyard. Let Brandr be jarl. Make Eindr stay, he'd be an excellent jarl. Me, I'd be a boat-builder.

But no, this is a good-bye. I've agreed to go with Ragnar, and he, for his part, has agreed to pay for two dozen men to stay behind for a year–this last not as a bride-price but as a kind of deposit on these very ships we build for the war. For his war.

Even though it's not in a marriage-bed, my fate is wedded to Ragnar's.

Rota is straining not to beg to come, but I already have a promise to stay and help. Kara said something cryptic while redoing my hair. Brandr weeps a little with his farewell and calls me grand-daughter, and it's true he loves me like one.

"Brandr," I begin. I've practiced this. "Kara is to act as jarl in my stead. This will, I hope, root her here in this world. She's drifting too far away. Also see to it that none of Ragnar's men touch her. I'm counting on you for this." And I have his word.

And so soon after I arrived at this village as a refugee, I leave as jarl. I've joined Ragnar's war for a share of silver, so that I can pay for his crew to remain in the Gaular, or find another to replace them. But by the gods, I will garrison the place for my people, one way or another.

The dapple will stay with the village, but Ragnar has found me another horse, a beautiful animal of dark chestnut. Eindr hands me the reins and offers me a hand, and I'm grateful for it as this creature is taller than I'm used to. It's wider too, so my hips hurt at first.

Ragnar hasn't said much. I don't think he's upset with me, or maybe he was but is less so when I agreed to go with him. His mind is heavy, I think.

So we ride, the eighty of us, north alongside the ridge where old Gudrunn and her bronze bell look down on us. North to where his boats are beached and watched by a small crew who've camped and fished these few weeks.

There are cheers as crew are reunited, deep kisses from some of the men awarded to the women among us, though some of these rebuked with good humour or a stiff thump to the chest. Not all, though. It's short enough work, fires lit and some last cooking while the boats are dragged over the stuttering rocks to the river, clear and cold from the last of the snow-melt.

Blocks of beeswax passed up and down to smooth edges, waterproof exposed folds in cloth, or to write runes of blessing or obscenity. The heavier men lean well overboard on the riverside as the horses embark, shushed and coaxed with apples, hands over their eyes until they are secure, side by side, into the familiar swaying. Bales of dried fish and strips of rabbit and other game, casks of tree-pitch and buckets of sand all packed in so there seems no room for crew at all, and here I find some use for myself, checking rigging, unfouling ropes, stowing and coiling. My hands know boats, and I want to be useful.

When the oars hit the water they do so in unison, and only then is the full perfection of the craft obvious. The boats draw hardly any water, so they perch on its surface like a bug. Only much, much swifter.

An hour, they say. An hour and this river meets the broader one, where we can raise the sail and make our way to the sea. At the thought of this, the green and salt of the ocean, I come alive in a way I'd thought long buried, my father's stories of the pirate queen Alfhild settling again in my heart. Alfhild, daughter of Siward–that can't be right. Another Siward, another Danish king. Ragnar's grandfather? Could Ragnar be descended from the heroine of my father's story? I'll have to ask him.

But the chatter and grunts of the rowers fall eerily silent, and as I look up to investigate, I see that I'm alone in the boat.

Alone in the whole world.

The others have vanished.

Gone too, are the other boats, and there's only myself, and this one skeith, and the river.

It's something maybe Kara could explain.

Then a sound, soft but strong, a wingbeat of a single, white swan, arrow-swift overhead and low.

The world now restored, crew and boats and gossip and singing, swearing and boasting and the creak of rope and wood and the slice and glide of oars.

That swan. I remember her from the beach, the fires of the huts reflected in her feathers.

"You haven't seen her yet?" Kara asks in memory. *"Soon, though. You'll see."*

And then another *her* for seeing. A girl, perhaps ten, black hair a-tangle, stares out at the boats from the river bank.

The wolf's-head girl from the forest. I'd swear to it.

A handful of hours to sail past the site of my old village. I can't look to the shore as we make our way past it. I don't know which would lay heavier on my heart: to see its charred ruins, or to see those few who remained having rebuilt some of it. Either way, it's the grave of my mother, my father. My self.

The speed fixates me. Nearly a week overland through forest, with outlaws and wolves and sore backs from sleeping on tree roots, all that distance dispensed with by a few hours of oar and sail. Impossible that anything can move this fast. And south to meet the rest of the fleet.

I'm not sure what I'll find there. Ragnar hasn't spoken of it, nor is there much talk of war here–just reunion, mostly. One owes another some weight in silver, or ale, and is either dreading or anticipating repayment.

When I first see them, I think it's some mistake. Some trick of the light. I try counting masts, sails, but then one bobs behind another and my brain can't make sense of them, or some flutter of oars and I have to start over.

"How many ships in the fleet?" I ask aloud to anyone listening.

One rower stops, cocks his head, squints. Counts thumb-tip to knuckle, twelve a hand and begins again. "Thirty-two, looks like, not counting the little ones."

Thirty-two ships. Each with between forty and sixty rowers, or if it's a buss then that's another hundred. Somewhere between twelve hundred and almost two thousand warriors. And these able to land anywhere in the Nordvegr in less than a day, or cross the sea to Sjeland or Jutland in another.

What can stand against such a fleet? I catch myself with my mouth open and laugh. I grip the rope tighter and pull myself up until I'm standing on the gunwales, something my father would chide me for but this... this is amazing.

A horn. Another. A cheer. It's for Ragnar, the son of their fallen king Siward, and curses for the rowers of Birka and Uppsala.

We beach the skeith and the two knarr, the men shirtless but with the silk striped breaches in gaudy colours instantly soaked by the sea. They haul and drag until the keel catches sand.

Ashore, the haggling begins, inventory taken and traded, promises made and contracts entered. Which hands to which ship under whose command. Signals and flags, strategies and stories.

But I have business of my own.

When I set out this morning, I had no glimmer of this idea. Skathi, goddess of the tide, who provided for my family and lulled me to sleep at night with slow shushing beat of her heart, cast this plan on the shore of myself.

So now I have a move to make.

Ragnar is there, squatting on the beach with men, drawing shapes in the sand with a stick. I'm reminded of the uncles planning farms on the dirt floor of my hall in the Gaular. But this is a plan for war, for rumours, sightings, local tides and currents, and this army of stories of this cliff, that bay, this beach.

"Ragnar," I say quietly. He raises a hand to silence the others and rises. He comes to me, smiling, and takes my arm. Eyes glower from bearded faces at this girl who dares interrupt the affairs of men.

One small boat, perhaps just a fishing boat, tacks sharply away from the fleet and heads southward with purpose. I'm not sure why I notice this, but it's something. News to bear, or some disagreement. But swift.

"You're having fun," I say. His smile broadens.

"I suppose I am," he says. "Are you?"

"Ragnar," I begin. "When you handed me my sword you said it was worth a kingdom."

"An expression." His characteristic shrug.

"Yes, but still," I say, serious. "I told you to sell me one."

"I offered you a kingdom, Ladda. But you won't marry me." He's not hurt by this. I think he is still flirting with me.

"So, sell me a kingdom, Ragnar. My own. I give you the sword, and you give me the ships and men I arrived with."

He thinks about this.

"A skeith and two knarr? With over a hundred warriors. I can't part with these."

I'm ready for his resistance. "So don't part with them. Just place them under my command."

"You already have a share, Ladda, for the boats you're building." He begins to walk, so we have some distance from the others on the beach. I take it to mean he's considering it, so I walk with him.

"I know," I say. "But I want boats in the water now."

He sees the sense of it, sees, as well, my need for it. "You think they'll follow you?"

"They'll follow me if I pay them."

"You'll have to pay them from your share," he agrees.

"I know how this works, Goat Pants," I say, laughing.

"King Goat Pants," he replies. "We almost have a deal."

"Oh?"

"I'll need a kiss," he says.

I sigh dramatically, playfully, and tap my cheek. He pecks there and seems satisfied. A final laugh, and he returns to his circle in the sand.

For my part, I have a crew to provision for.

Night, and the rowers at rest just offshore. Some of the ships have been tied together, and there's music that accompanies the slap of the water against the hull. A leather tent has been set up on the deck, but the rain has held off, even though the sky darkened with more than nightfall. Most sleep, but others drink, clatter knucklebones against the hull and cheer or swear. Some pray quietly, some snore.

There are things beneath us in the black water, awake or asleep, capable of erasing us from Midgard in a single swipe or swallow. Serpents beneath the world, always. Not tonight. Or not hungry for us, at least.

The sound of a rowboat rises over the sound of distant singing, and it's Ragnar. It's bright enough from torches that I can see the blonde of his scruffy beard. I can see, too, that he's smiling.

"King Goat Pants comes to honour us with his rowing!" I call to him.

"Ladda! I hardly recognized you," he teases. "I thought it was the ghost of the pirate queen, Alfhild."

"And I thought she was your grandmother," I answer cheekily.

"Grandmother? No, but something of a family legend."

"Wife or daughter of Siward, I thought," I tell him, taking the rope he tosses me. I secure the line to the gunwales and pretend I don't notice him admiring the knot.

"So many Siwards in my family I can't keep track," he says, climbing aboard. "I'm surprised I'm not one."

"But Ragnar, 'the ruler,'" I say. "Your parents had plans for you."

"Or Ragnarok, the end of the world," he teases. "Dark plans, maybe."

"Why have you come to see me, World-Ender?"

"Our bargain," he says.

"What? I let you kiss me already," I say, surprised. I expect he's here for another. Or more.

"You kept my sword," he says, grinning.

"That I did," I admit. I had forgotten. I had removed it earlier, placed it in the center of a bundle with woolen cloak and my traveling things. Spoon and board and comb, the wolf skin which I haven't needed since the wind died down.

I hand him the beautiful thing; its steel seems to glow dimly in the moonlight.

"This concludes our deal," I say formally.

"We'll drink, then," he suggests.

"You'll have to row back to your own boat."

"Do I?"

"Yes, Ragnar, you do." I don't like where this is going, if he decides to be stubborn.

"One drink then," he says. "I can row on one horn of wine."

"Wine?" I mock him. "What Frankish galley is this, Ragnar? We have ale, or mead. And I'd have to steal the mead."

"Ale then, thanks," he says. Gods, the boy is beautiful. And the freedom of the day, the speed of the boats–my boats–south into the darkening sea, this has my blood up. But I suspect Ragnar could be difficult to get rid of.

I lie. I don't suspect it, I know it.

A stoppered jar fills the horn he pulls from his belt, and he doesn't look away as he downs the thing. A sadness crosses his face, just for an instant.

"What?" I ask.

"My father," he says, perching on the gunwales, steading himself with a rope and taking care not to rattle the axe handles hanging there. "I barely knew him, hardly remember him as a child. But in the end, he brought me here. With you."

"His death, you mean."

"I was born here, you know. In the north. My father went to raid, and while away, a man—his friend—Ring, seized the throne, so there was a war. I was taken away to Birka, and raised there in hiding."

"You're no Swede," I say to him.

"No, but my father had allies there. And with his lands in Jutland, he had supporters. So, we made a plan to conspire with Ring against my father, and I was supposed to be Ring's puppet."

"But it was a trap," I say.

"It was a trap. We earned Ring's trust, and I betrayed him, securing my father's throne," he says, like he's reciting something. He swallows the mead, a little trickle in his beard he wipes away with the back of his hand.

"How?"

"How? I murdered him," he says plainly.

"How old were you?"

"Thirteen."

Suddenly I think of Kara, jarl for just a day but still only twelve years old. What have I done to her?

"Then what happened?" I ask, trying to distract myself.

"We returned to Jutland. To Heithabyr, and my father's lands there. It was the only time I had with him. But he had business in the north, and was here when Fro invaded. My father was killed in battle. So," he says, taking another drink, "I sail to avenge his death."

"A Norwegian prince, raised by Swedes, with a Danish army, searching for a Swedish king." I think I need a drawing in the sand to keep track of all this.

"A tangle," he nods. "The gods choose these things for us." He reaches out and touches my hair gently.

"All right, Goat Pants," I take his hand from my head, press it into his own chest. "Back you go."

"So soon?"

"My ship, my rules. I'll have you thrown overboard." I'm only half-kidding.

"I am the king, you know."

"You are the king of the Nordvegr," I say, pointing at the shore. "You'll have to swim for it."

"Not a bad night for a swim," he says.

"Don't tempt me," I reply.

"That's why I came here," he laughs.

"You think I don't know that?" I'm not upset with him, but he doesn't understand. "The men, Ragnar. They can't see me as your woman. They have to see me as their commander and in no other way."

He shrugs. "You are right as always, Jarl Hladgertha." He steps with one long stride over the side of the skeith and into his rowboat. "But it was worth trying."

I untie the knot, toss the rope to him. He catches it without looking.

"Ragnar," I say, as his boat begins to wobble away. "Garrison my village, and I'll make you king. In reality, not just in name. That's our only deal now."

"Make me king," he says, raising the sword slightly, "and I'll make you rich."

Dawn snaps the sails awake, and within minutes of stretching, groaning, stowing, and pissing overboard, my three ships have rows in the water. The sun is already warm, with the wind a chill behind us, though the horizon still lies under a leaden sky.

To war then, tomorrow if not today.

There is no plan. If we discover Fro's fleet in the water, we attack them. If we see them beached, we take as many of their boats as we can. If no sign, we take to shore and find a high point to see what we can. This is a hunt. We're steady, and look for tracks.

After an hour of rowing, we pull the oars aboard and the crew breaks fast. There's little talk among them. The grey seeps towards us, and even warmed by labour, we are chilled by sweat, so cloaks are unbundled, pinned, adjusted. Jars of fresh water passed along the line.

The fleet is spread out and ragged in such times, subject to the fickle nature of wind. It doesn't matter much—south, south is all that counts. Across the sea to Jutland, as the Nordvegr falls away at our stern.

This, I can only guess, is the main thing of war. The waiting. The routine. To meet the demands of the ship after each creak or groan, after the slip of the tide, the shift of the wind. Serve the ship, which serves the sea, to serve the war.

On my signal the fleet takes to oar again, like a single animal. A cat stretching in the sun. In moments, the fleet again is a line, barely a ship's width between each oar-tip. And then back to the relentless rhythm and the speed and spit of salt.

South to the sea. The sea and the darkening sky.

It's the rumble, first. And each of us knows its meaning.

Thunder. The gods are coming.

When the lightning flashes in the distance, it's almost an absurdity. Black outlines of masts, sail-less beneath the storm our own ships have yet to greet. The enemy, far sooner than any of us could have expected. The sea white-capped and choppy, no current we can make out. Backs groan into each pull of the oar. A woman, slight as myself, scrambles barefoot up the mast to slip the yard and drop our own sail.

"Hold!" I shout. She looks around at the faces of the men, for signs of support or defiance.

"I said hold!" I yell over the rising wind. "We keep our speed as long as we can. There's the line. We sail for it. Now row!"

War is not new to me, I realize. I've seen it. Seen the faces of the slayer and the slain. My own face has worn defeat, and vengeance. I have slogged with my people through misery and grief, I have known blisters from spear and the spray of hot blood on my hands and face. I won't be dismissed by men who row boats paid by my own silver, my own debts, my own oaths. And despite all I know of war, I know boats better.

Speed is force. And the wind is with us, at least until it tears us apart. I can work with that.

Another lightning strike, another forest of masts burned into and out of sight. Impossible to count but greater numbers than our own. Twice? Impossible, as I say, everything's moving, tangling in vision.

I look to the boats in our line, and we're more or less the right flank of it, seaward. The line holds. Ragnar means to sail right into them, a frontal assault, so long as the wind is with us, though ship after ship drops sail as the wind becomes increasingly dangerous.

But our sails are up, despite what the storm is throwing at us. As a result, my three ships are now in advance of the line, the wind giving us additional speed. If we are the first to slam into them, we'll just be the first to die.

I have a plan.

I can't shout over the wind. There are flags, but I don't know what they mean and I'm embarrassed to ask how to use them. I can only trust my other two captains, whose names I can't even remember, will follow.

Gods, let them follow.

I scramble to the stern, shins banging against each thwart, half-swinging from stays. I greet the steersman, wet from spray, and point. His arms are like roots of some great tree, and he throws their strength into the starboard. We wheel away from our own fleet, breaking seaward to flank the enemy line.

Gods, let them follow.

And they do. My three ships are with me, sails now straining now luffing against the storm, whipping as loud as the thunder.

Fro's line holds. None peel off to meet us, as I had feared. Or would have feared, had I thought of it until now. It is only a few minutes until we are nearly alongside them, though well off from the left flank of their fleet.

Nothing but ocean behind us. Between us and the shore more ships and axes than I can count. Than I could have imagined this morning.

I haul myself up on the stays so that I can be seen by my other ships, pointing south-west, out to nothing. Pointing hard. We row, and keep a line of our own. Now past and west of the navy which closes fast upon our friends.

I'm waving my arms now, shouting. I point southeast, as though the fury of my pointing could shift the wind, shift the current, as if by my will alone I can bend three ships at once to a new fate.

The rain is soaking us as we are under the full fury of the storm. I point to the woman who has not moved from the mast, and she climbs, understanding, up to the halyard line, descending again on the rope as the yard begins to come down. Likewise, my two knarr drop sail, and we're all rowing now. Rowing for our lives.

This is it, two thirds of a wheel, with only the hardest to do as we fight the sea to come 'round the rear of Fro's forces. We grind our oar blades into the salt, seemingly to go nowhere. Harder then, all of us, muscles burning, skin tearing from hands on oars and ropes, throats roaring just to turn, turn east, turn 'round. And with each stroke, a small victory, though the storm itself resents us.

Painfully slowly and hard won, it is working, with a line kept and now we are directly behind the Swedish navy, seventy boats by quick counting, in a strict line. Arrows fly northward from the fleet into Ragnar's line. We know some are already dying.

"I curse you," I mutter at first. "Fro, wolf of Birka and Uppsala, I curse you."

I make my way to the bow.

"Fro, hear me. I come for you. I, Hladgertha, daughter of the mother whose face you cut with an axe, daughter of the father you cut down in the night, I curse you. I am coming to kill you."

My voice is rising. I nearly give in to the hypnotic rhythm of my own dark song, when an idea hits me like a blow to the back, the hair on my neck standing. I look around. Buckets. Barrels of pitch. Buckets of sand. Buckets for bailing.

"Water!" I yell. "Seawater in those buckets, now!"

Oarsmen drop what they are doing, throw the buckets overboard with the ropes attached and drag them back full.

I myself grab a small cask of pitch, used to seal planks, and begin painting the gunwales. It is madness, and no one understands. How could they?

"Soak the sails!" The men get to it, dousing the sails, now on deck yet still wadded to the yard, returning the buckets to the sea, and repeating. I've covered the front third of the boat with pitch and a rag.

"Get that sand ready, and for the sake of the gods, keep the water away when I say so, or we will all burn!"

They stare at me blankly, until I take the rag to the coal fire in the iron pot at the center of the boat, holding flame in my hand. I light the pitch and drop the rag overboard, though not before feeling the flame's heat crack my skin like a whip.

The gunwales of my own ship are on fire.

I have set my own ship on fire.

"Row!" I scream, shrill and mad in what I've done, the crew terrified that I've killed them already, or resigned to the fact.

"Fro!" I shout. "I curse you. I Hladgertha, who have survived you, curse you. The gods curse you. The fates curse you. The spirits of my family look at you from Valhalla and deny you. You die this day and you will never enter the hall of your forefathers! You will wander the depths of the sea and the fish themselves will shun you!"

We are upon the enemy. I see the faces of Fro's men, turning and horrified at every sailor's worst nightmare. Fire at sea.

"Odinn sees you with one eye and looks away!" The flames rumble like the thunder, like the wind. "Thor sees you and strikes lightning upon you. Freya gazes upon your ugliness with disgust and vomits! Heimdallr sounds not the Gjallarhorn and closes the bifrost to you! The Valkyries fly over your slain and cooling corpse and do nothing! I curse you, Fro, leech-worm and frost-bitten toe! I curse you to Hel!"

The boats tack and scramble, spin sideways as one whole row of their oars stop to grab water or sand.

The rear of Fro's line breaks, scattered, panicked. We have cut the enemy in two.

"Oars up!" We're close enough now. Any more and our oars would tangle with theirs. "Archers!" and short bows appear from under the thwarts. Some stand, others fire from where they are sitting but the backs of the rowers in front of us are easy targets, and our forty warriors fell a hundred, two, in an instant. The sky is full like the flight of starlings as our arrows find the enemy.

"Sand!" I scream. "Keep the water away from the pitch of or the fire will spread!"

Half the crew fights the fire I started, while the others pound relentlessly into the enemy, shot after shot after shot. The fire is soon out, with the help of some hides my crew have the sense to apply. I don't know if I've damaged the ship or if I've merely scorched the wood.

I also don't know how this axe appeared in my hand, just like that day on the beach.

There is a gigantic groan of hull on hull, as we grind alongside a knarr of the enemy. A dozen of my warriors already aboard, swinging axes into the foe.

The hull is too round, and I can't make the jump from where I'm standing on the bow. There's a kind of bridge between our smaller ship and the larger one of the enemy's, but it's a bridge we hold, we own, and we pour across it like blood through a wound.

And I'm aboard their ship, my axe gone, buried in the chest of a man who has vanished into the sea with it. I have my shield, left hand in the boss and right hand, still singing with pain, on the rim the bottom edge finding knee, back, throat, skull.

Slamming warriors between my shield's edge and their own hulls. Over and over.

My voice is an animal thing now. The caw of a raven. It is the scratch of a talon on the wind. My arm is glowing with pain, yet there is no thought to stopping, none to mercy, and even less to fatigue. I can't see out of my left eye, as salt from blood spray has glued it shut.

"Ladda," a voice says. "Ladda!"

And I wheel around to crush the throat that dares hold my name.

But Ragnar is quick. He's unarmed and simply plucks the shield from me. I'm shaking and weak. How long have I been like this?

The rain continues, but the sounds of battle are over.

"Ragnar?" my voice is almost nothing. A ghost of salt and burnt skin.

"You have the ship, Ladda. Your men have been trying to speak to you."

I look around and see faces, some triumphant, joyous, others in shock from their own wounds or loss of comrades. I know that look.

"You're hurt," Ragnar says, pointing to my eye.

"It's not my blood," I tell him, still hoarse. "At least, I don't think so."

"Fro is dead, Ladda. The fleet is broken. We've taken most of it, and the others have fled east."

I nod.

"East," I repeat.

"It's over. We won." Ragnar dabs the blood from my eye with a wet cloth, though it doesn't seem to help.

"Won," I say. I'm still confused. A ghost. What happened? I was on this ship, there was a battle, and then the battle was over.

"The storm has swung westward. We'll tie the ships together and tend the wounded, then make for shore. Each ship will be short-handed, so it will take some doing."

"We lost so many?" I ask.

"We doubled the fleet, Hladgertha."

I nod, seeing the practicality of it. More ships, fewer hands.

And then I turn over the side and vomit. Ragnar is holding my hair, my long hair down my back, matted and crusted with blood. He's laughing.

"Ladda?" Ragnar says. "You set your own ship on fire." And then he laughs even louder at the sheer insanity of it. "Your own ship! On fire!"

And I'm laughing too now, though coughing and spitting at the same time, wiping my eye with my good hand and spittle from my chin on my sleeve.

"I did," I laugh, still barely with any voice. "I set my ship on fire!"

And what hurts most now is my ribs from laughing. That and I've probably broken one.

— PART II —

Hjorring. I couldn't have imagined such a place.

The hall, I think, could contain every house I've ever been in, and there are stone walls everywhere. An hour spent building a wall is an hour less in the fields or fishing, so I can't understand how a village so huge can feed itself. There are men who are paid to do nothing all day but stand, with spear and shield, and look intimidating.

We sit at the great table, with every corner capped by some bit of bronze, beautifully inscribed. Each surface polished, straightened, gleaming, throwing candlelight back at us even though it's mid-day.

I'm the only woman here. Even the servants who bring Frankish wine to the table and replenish our silver cups are men.

Ragnar found me a new dress—war has again claimed what I was wearing—this one green with a gold apron, banded by some white fabric that is softer than the finest wool and shimmers in the light.

It took all night to wash the blood from my hair, and I wear it in a single plait down my back.

We talk of the spoils of war. What lands of Fro's have to be raided to compensate for losses, what treasure from what ship goes to which jarl. And of course, taxes to the king.

"Why do you get taxes?" I whisper to Ragnar while the other men argue.

"Shh. As a jarl, you get your share, too." He winks at me.

"Jarl?" says one older man. His name is Caldr, and he sneers at everything. I try not to laugh at his nose hairs, which reach down to his beard. "Jarl of what? Three huts covered in goat shit, north of nowhere. This girl does not get a jarl's tax."

There's some laughter and snorting at this. Rorik, the jarl from the beach that day my village fell, watches my face calmly. Ragnar too says nothing.

"Four," I say.

"What?" This Caldr is dimwitted as he is rude.

"I'm the jarl of *four* huts covered in goat shit. Not three." This is met by more laughter.

"Further," I continue, "I am the jarl of three ships, one of which I set on fire to break Fro's line and turn the tide of battle when we were outnumbered two to one. I am the jarl that lets you drink and laugh today instead of having your flesh snapped off in fish teeth. So, yes, your debt to me is not a jarl's tax. Your debt to me is your life."

He glares at me, but there are approving nods from the others. He won't pursue this.

"So, Ladda," says Ragnar, as though none of this has taken place, "what do you want?"

"Seven," I say. I've been thinking through this all night, wishing I had Brandr to consult with, Rota to talk to, Kara to baffle me with talk of gods and elves. "Seven ships, and the silver to pay the crew."

There is some coughing and sputtering at this.

"That," adds Ragnar, "is a great share."

"It is," I agree. "But I was a tenth of our fleet, so I get a tenth of theirs."

"Will the men even follow you, if we granted you this?" asks Caldr.

"Crew. Not all are men, Jarl Caldr," I correct him. "And you grant me nothing. I claim this as my right." Again, some nods.

"And what would you do with these men?" Caldr is still trying to get some kind of rise from me.

"Crew," I correct him again.

He shrugs.

"I'm sending two ships home to garrison my village, to help build and bring in the harvest."

"Two ships? Eighty men. We cannot spare their shields, or backs, or axes." Caldr again.

Rorik intervenes. He's been quiet this whole time, but he's smiling with his eyes.

"Perhaps," he begins, "Jarl Hladgertha can spare her... crew, for a set time. We agree to award her her spoils, she keeps the fleet together, and is compensated by a modest share, so that we can continue to raid in compensation."

"I..." I begin, objecting.

"Jarl Hladgertha will consider this," interrupts Ragnar with some finality. "I'm sure she will give us her answer this evening. But it is a fair offer, Jarl Rorik."

I'm fuming at being cut off like that, but I can tell that both Rorik and Ragnar are looking out for me. I struggle with my temper and diffuse it somewhat by looking at Caldr with contempt. That, I realize, is highly satisfying.

Ragnar seems to have concluded the meeting, but the men still talk amongst themselves. Trading goods, grazing lands, fishing rights, river access. The loan of a master boatbuilder, introductions, marriage arrangements.

And this I see now is the real business of the thing. Each deal is like part of a ship, the conversations and agreements mast, sails, rigging. This betrothal an oar, this trade a starboard. Every scrap of claimed land, each islet and jarldom, part of a single boat that sails forward, feeds the crew. It's dizzying to see so clearly how the world works.

I rise to leave, in need of air, and Ragnar too swings one leg lazily over the bench to join me. I'm not in the mood for company. We walk past the men whose job it is to stand there for no reason, and they pretend we're not there. Somehow this has something to do with Ragnar being king, I suppose. That he is too important to be actually seen by mere warriors. I don't know. It's confusing but also funny to think of.

"Rorik's idea is a good one," Ragnar says, matching my stride. I'm not headed anywhere in particular.

"I don't recall asking for your advice," I tell him, perhaps too sharply.

"Me either," he says, teasing. "But still, you should consider it."

"I will," I tell him.

"You should consider it and then reject it," he says.

I'm surprised. "Why?"

"Because I'll pay you more to come with me," Ragnar says.

I stop and turn to him. "What are you talking about?"

"Rorik was just trying to get Caldr to shut up. He always knows what to say."

"So?" I'm still snapping. I suppose I'm just tired.

"So, you have ten ships, and I have another war to fight. I'll match Rorik's suggestion. You get the ships and silver for the crew, plus a little more for coming with me and not returning to the Gaular this year."

"But I thought you needed to keep the fleet together to raid Fro's lands?"

"Later, maybe. We'll see." He doesn't seem to care.

"So what war are you fighting then?"

"Harald," he says.

Bloody Hel, I think. More workings of this machine I've never heard of. "And he is?"

"One of my father's advisors, who I convinced to work with Ring against my father."

"So you could betray him," I say, remembering.

"Yes, but it seems Harald is very good at betrayal. He now says that he is the king of the Jutland. And Sjeland."

"So did he really serve Ring, only pretending to serve you?" I'm catching up, slowly.

"He serves himself. That just makes him human. I don't blame him."

"But you intend to kill him."

"Of course," he says, smiling. "It's war."

I pause, just to watch his smile fade a little in uncertainty. Just a bit. "I could just take my ships and go home," I say.

"You could. If you want to. But that would buy you a year, perhaps, a year I've already paid for. And next winter you would have the same problem. If you come with me, you will have enough silver for many winters. You have no idea how much money is in the south, and further south."

Just looking at Hjorring, at all the activity around me, I can't imagine greater wealth. Everything is in rows. So much bronze, and silver ornamentation even outside where any night-thief or wolf's-head could come in the dark and pry it loose. Even the barns are stone, instead of stave.

"Why me? You know I won't marry you, Ragnar."

"I know. But we make a good team, Ladda, you and I. Besides, Eindr says you are a goddess."

I nearly spit at the absurdity of it.

"What?"

"Oh yes. He thinks you are Thorgertha, from the sagas. So our victory is assured when you sail with us." He's not laughing but I can tell he wants to.

"If I was of the gods I suspect they'd make more sense to me," I say.

"If Eindr says you are Thorgertha, then the others say you are Thorgertha. And that is a valuable thing. Now if we can only get the enemy to say it." He's laughing now, but he's not mocking me. "Of course," he adds, "Eindr is in love with you."

"What? No! Ragnar!" It has been a day of disbelief thus far. I punch his arm.

"Oh yes. You can't tell? Rorik is in love with you, too. You should marry him. He's very rich."

"You can't be serious," I reply. It's all a bit much.

"Whatever you say," shrugs Ragnar, wandering off now. "You're the goddess."

By the time I re-enter the hall of Hjorring, the men are deep into the wine. So, too, are the women, who have spent the day with their own market of exchanges, glances, rumours, and deals. The air is slowly thickening with smoke, and while there's some sweat in it, and the scent of fish, there is also perfume; warm cedar and ambergris.

There's a place for me, there, at the high table, but it's currently occupied. Thora, the daughter of one of Caldr's men, though not of Caldr himself, I think. She's pretty, and she laughs easily. Ragnar can't stop looking at her, which bothers me. As her foot reaches out to touch his leg, it bothers me more, though I should not care. I turn away.

Eindr.

At a table, he's lit by candles, perhaps a dozen. I've never seen so many candles so close together before. It's as though he sits in a tiny island of sunlight.

There are markings on the page of the thinnest goat-skin, but they're not runes. Flowing lines, like water. Lines not to be inscribed into wood or stone, but to be painted with ink from a green jar, chased in gold. Eindr uses a goose feather to imitate the small black strokes before him.

"What is it?" I ask. It's beautiful.

"Arabic, Jarl Hladgertha," Eindr says, rising.

"Ladda," I remind him. "Please don't stop. I didn't mean to interrupt you."

He smiles and sits down again, arranging the pages.

"I don't know what that is," I confess. "This Arabic."

"I am just learning, myself. A language. A people, far to the south and east." His words are crisp, patient. I can make out the light of fresh oils in the curls of his hair as I lean closer to him.

"Saxons?" I guess, remembering.

"Far, far beyond the Saxons," he tells me with a smile.

"The world is so big, then?"

"It is, Jarl Hladgertha." He swallows. "Ladda."

"And these?" I point at the pages on the table.

"Writing. Contracts. This word, here, see?" he says, pointing. "*Rus.*"

"What is Rus?" I ask.

"Us. All of us, any people who row in ships. Jutlanders, Sjelanders, from the Nordvegr, the Vestfold, and Trondelag. Even the Gotar. The Svear."

"They think we're the same?" It's ridiculous to me.

"Anyone to their north who arrives by river, yes."

I'm still taking all this in, the wideness of the world and how some outsider can draw a circle around all I've known and say it's just one common thing. "But our gods, our words..." I protest.

"They do not trade in gods. We bring wool; we work iron. We sell slaves; we buy silk," he explains. "So, as far as their accounting goes, we are the same."

I'm honestly amazed at this.

"And you've been there?" I ask. "This Arabic?"

"No," he says. "Not yet. But once I have learned to read properly, I may assist Jarl Rorik with the contracts, and perhaps even learn to speak with them."

"Jarl Rorik? I thought you were with Ragnar?"

"I am in thrall to Jarl Rorik. I was born so," he says calmly.

"Thrall?" I'm taken off guard. "You're a slave?"

He nods, simply. "Yes."

Slaves, to me, were always farmers, and only for the rich who could afford them. But here is this man with kind brown eyes, dark-browed, soft-spoken, and learned. He is also adorned, in his Frankish robe, with silver rings. He looks rich.

"You dress like a Frank," I say.

"Jarl Rorik insists," he explains. "There is much money to be made in dealing with the Franks."

"Tell me." As dizzying as this wider world is, I want more of it.

"This," he says, pulling a paper out from beneath his pile, "is Latin. Once a great empire, even south of the Franks." It's more like runes, I think. Each character distinct, better for carving, and not the looping inky line of Arabic.

"And the Franks use this Latin?"

"Only for some things. They do not speak it, but they write in it. To prove, I think, that they are their own empire now. Perhaps the richest in all the world. Their capital is Paris, an island surrounded by a wall so high the giants could not peer over it. But inside is so much gold that to look at it in the sun will blind a man."

"Good thing I'm a woman then," I grin. "I should take a peek."

Glancing over to the head table, I see that Rorik is, at the moment unaccompanied, by Caldr.

"Please excuse me," I say, and Eindr makes to rise again but I press his shoulders down to his work with a smile. He nods in subtle thanks, and only then do I remember Ragnar saying Eindr is in love with me.

Which brings me to Rorik. It's only a few steps, but it seems like there's a world between Eindr's island of light and this table.

"You're not taking your ships to raid Fro's lands," Rorik says, grinning as I approach. The man he had been talking to, slight with skin like leather, draws his hood over his face and recedes into the shadows.

"True. So how did you know I was going to say this?" I ask.

"I only suggested that you consider raiding the north to silence Caldr." He takes a sip from his cup. "As much as that can be done," he adds.

"Ragnar said as much."

"Then Ragnar also made you an offer," Rorik says, gesturing me to sit beside him. A girl comes to fill his cup, but he waves her away and pours the wine himself. Light glances off the gold on his fingers. "An offer he also made me." The whole thing seems to please him.

"And?" I ask, though I know already.

"And I'm coming south with you. With both of you, you and Ragnar."

"But you still didn't answer how you knew what I would say. I didn't tell Ragnar."

"Because, Jarl Hladgertha, or Ladda, if I may, seeing as we are to be partners in this venture," he says, "every moment I spend with you I see more of your character. It is the wise choice. In the best interest of your people. This keeps the fighting farther from them, and you are a good leader."

He sips again. "And good luck too, I think."

I catch myself smiling. It feels good, to have earned the respect of such men. And I must confess it is likewise satisfying to have earned the contempt of Caldr.

"Caldr won't like it."

"I'm sending him north. We'll see what happens. If he returns, so be it. If not, I pray to Odinn his sons will be more agreeable."

"You can send him, just like that?" Power seems marvellous.

"Caldr is feal to me, yes."

"As you are to Ragnar," I state.

"As we all are," he says. "To the king. Also, this Harald pretender has set up camp in my home."

"What?" I'm trying to dig out a map from my memory, Jutland and the Nordvegr and the Kattegat Sea.

"Yes, in Aalborg. And I mean to chase him out of it. I was hoping that one of my servants would have just poisoned him by now, to be honest. But perhaps they lack initiative. Anyway, I'm sure it will be a simple enough matter when we arrive."

"I've learned a lot today that I wasn't aware I didn't know," I tell Rorik. "But I think with my ships, and Ragnar's, and yours, that's thirty ships if no one else joins us, the fleet we faced Fro with. I'm guessing this Harald's forces will not be as much."

"It's a good guess," he says. "But I too would just be guessing."

"Well, you know the shore better, and the tides." I reach for his cup and take a sip. The cup itself is enormous, like a fist of silver. I put it back down.

"There is that. But they've been there long enough to get a grasp of things. And some are my own men, changing alliances."

"Complicated," I say.

"Business," he shrugs.

"A business you can die in," I remind him.

"Any worthwhile business, you can die in," he laughs. He raises his cup to me.

"I'm tired, Jarl Rorik," I tell him. I am, suddenly.

"No titles between friends, I think, Ladda." He half-whispers this, leaning towards me slightly. I catch his scent, and he smells good. Different from Ragnar. Sweeter. Like beeswax.

"Rorik, then." and I smile at him. "Tell Ragnar... where is Ragnar, anyway? He was right here."

"I believe he and the Princess Thora have their own business to conduct," he says.

"And die in," I answer, perhaps gruffly.

"As you say," Rorik nods. "But shall I tell him you're coming south with us?"

"Yes, you can tell him I accept his offer," I say, standing. "And tell him..."

"Yes?"

"Tell him I want my sword back."

Again the spray of salt and wind in my hair. Not my ship, not yet, but Ragnar's karv, a smaller nimble vessel best suited for inshore. There's a chill to the air the sun hasn't yet chased from the water.

"Where are Rorik's boats?" I ask Ragnar. "Why isn't he with us?"

"I don't know," Ragnar says, unconcerned. "Behind us. He will be there at the rally point."

The point has only been roughly described, but our twenty ships sail towards it. A headland just north of the entrance to the Limfjord, farther south than I've ever been, and not even half-way to Ragnar's hall at Heithabyr. *Just keep the beach to our left, and when the beach ends, that is the mouth of the fjord, more of an inland sea,* Ragnar had said. A round bay, leading to two rivers, with Aalborg first to the north, then on the easternmost shore. If Harald knows we're coming, he'll choke off the entrance to the bay and meet us with Greek fire, a kind of dragon's breath that pitches balls of flame ship to ship. When I ask Ragnar why we don't have this, he shrugs.

"Who would be on board with such a thing?" he asks.

"The enemy," I answer.

He doesn't seem to take the matter seriously, and I resist the urge to shove him overboard.

"What if we beach north of the mouth and march overland?" I suggest.

"It's a long walk," he says. "We lose speed. Also," he adds, "there is no open country past the beach. Small groups of archers can pick us off as we march inland. There would be none left alive by the time we got there."

"And to the south?"

"I don't know. I don't know this country."

"Which is why Rorik should be here," I add sharply.

"He should," Ragnar agrees, and changes the subject. "We'll get you to your ships soon."

I squint into the summer sun. How many months since that day on the river, leaving the Gaulardale? How many months since I've seen my siblings? My heart seems to stab itself with worry, particularly for Kara. I'm not sure I trust Ragnar's men. But I do trust Brandr, and I trust Rota to keep our sister safe.

Forest.

It took everything I had to leave my ships there, in the midst of battle. Harald knew we were coming, and tied his ships together into an island of war.

The tide had pushed much of this to the north, and bound up in a fortress were less maneuverable. So I left my seven, newly-won ships with Ragnar, and took my skeith and two karr,–one hundred and twenty warriors–to the south bank of the Limfjord, seemingly abandoning the fight.

We were ready for ships to break away from Harald's fleet to engage us, but either they didn't think of it, or couldn't. Whichever.

And here we are, half-running with shield and spear, leaving only twenty to fight and die for our beached ships. The last hundred of us raking air into our lungs, eyes wide for any sign of the enemy.

How many hours north? None of us knows. Rorik might, and could tell us if he hadn't disappeared. Maybe some rogue fleet of Harald's got to them before the rally point, and it wounds me to think of him dead.

Could I love him?

He's, what, charming? Yes. Rich? Of course. And there is a confidence to him that doesn't cross into Ragnar's arrogance and seeming laziness. I'm unkind. Ragnar isn't arrogant, he just seems trusting in his *orleg* as king. Wedded to the gods as he is, he can seem unapproachable, or at least, impenetrable. Rorik on the other hand, impressive, yes, but still with a man's vulnerabilities.

Where in Hel is my head? Right now, we march and stay alert. All this green sets my mind wandering, and I have a body to stay in if I wish to keep it breathing throughout the day. Belts are wrapped in swaths of cloth to keep gear from rattling. We're single file and moving fast.

A scout returns from the left advance, following a ridgeline above the fjord. He sees smoke that might be Aalborg. Two mil, maybe more. If we push, we'll make it by sunset.

We're betting on the place being unguarded, with all hands to Harald's fleet. But we have no way of knowing. If we're wrong, we can recede into the forest, south, but no way, really, back to our boats. So we'll either take the hall, or be scattered, walking home. None of this instills me with confidence, but for whatever reason I'm not afraid.

I'm too stubborn to be afraid.

This explains the scars on my knees from when I was little, the scar too under my chin, now pale-white and all but invisible but once red and glaring for a whole year. Too stubborn now to stop and rest, knowing we are racing the sun, with five hours to go before the battle can even begin.

A branch nearly takes my eye out of carelessness. I swear and struggle to keep up with the column.

There's no time to pause when we see the village. No time for orders as the forest falls away. We are lean and hungry and sore, but without cover and with the suddenness of clearing, we have one choice.

We run at them.

Howling, we run. Praying, we run. Cursing, we run. But we run. With shield and spear and short bow we loose whatever we can upon the enemy, which at this point is merely the sides of some buildings, some goat-herds, and some startled men who look around on the ground for wherever it was they placed leather helmets. We're upon them.

We've stumbled on a terrace above the village proper, and it gives us good vantage on the place. Mercifully, it's probably half-empty. Comically, we realize the area is huge. Hjorring would probably fit on this perch on which we find ourselves.

I wave scouts ahead, although we've been seen and shouts of warning ring through the town below. As the sun sets, I can see well up the river, to the battle still raging, ship to ship. We've caught most of the residents gazing out to sea.

What I assumed to be the great hall is merely a barn, given the traffic of cattle going into it. The hall itself is some distance away and has a roof of beam and wood, not of earth. Iron and bronze reflect pink light, as rivets and mail, shield and spear are brought into a line between us and it. And beyond the hall, down to the water, the docks we must take.

If we take the docks—and hold them—we take any resupply ships that leave the battle. If the docks fall to us, Aalborg falls. Harald falls.

"Archers!" I call, and forty, sixty warriors are at my back at a word, the creak of bowstring a chorus.

I cut the air with my sword, and scores of black feathers fill the sky like a hail of crows.

Another volley, and another, are loosed before the first arrows hit a disciplined wall of shields. As the storm continues, however, here a shield falls. Another.

Another.

And with a thrust of my sword, I am a rock in a river of women and men, leaping, joyous, shrieking, growling as they pour around me in a torrent toward the shield wall. Their return fire is sporadic, a spitting of arrows, yet each shot more effective than ours—our shields are not up to catch them. I race behind the crest of the tide I have unleashed.

One hundred against so many. They're fed and rested. They know the land, each rock and ankle-tearing hollow. We have only our shields and axes, our fury, and the speed of running downhill.

It's chaos. There is no wall-to-wall of wood with spears overhead. It's a pit where the back to yours could be crewmate or foe. You fight only what you can see.

This spear-arm is too open on the thrust, so I duck a little and stab into the armpit. This neck is exposed for a heartbeat between collar and helm, so I thrust there and the heart beats crimson into the ground. Low, there is an unprotected hamstring on a lunge, so I reach out and snap it, drawing back. Simple. Where there's metal, I dodge from it. Where there's flesh, I stab at it. The rest is madness and rage and fire in the blood.

There's a sound like singing, or like the peal of a bell, incredibly close. Then everything is black for an instant.

On my back, I can taste the blood, my cheek hot like I've been branded. I prop myself up on my left elbow, pain stabbing through my shoulder, and touch my face with my right hand.

There is blood, and pain, and ringing, and the setting of the sun.

And then there's nothing.

Water. Not of the shore or a river. But a basin. The wringing of a cloth and the pressing of a bruise. I'm awake.

Smoke. A warrior dabs blood from my face, not aware or not caring his own could use the same attention. A red beard I recognize, the man who pulled me to my feet a lifetime ago in the Gaulardale.

I should have expected Valkyries, I'm thinking.

"Shh," he says, stopping my hand from my face. "Spear shaft. Point's taken a bit of your ear, hence all the blood. Nothing bleeds like an ear. And the shaft itself has given your cheek a good pummeling. Can't tell if it's broken, though."

I probe my tongue into my cheek. Pain, but it's not that bad.

He reads my eyes. "No? All right in a week, then, Jarl Ladda. Maybe two."

"Where are we?" I ask. It's dark, and few fires where we are.

"Where you fell, in the field behind the hall. The rest are inside."

"The rest?" I prop myself up on one elbow, and the world is nearly white with pain. I try the other one, and it leans me away from my red-bearded caregiver.

"Half. Maybe." He says, grimly.

"But?" I'm looking for news.

"Aalborg is yours, Jarl Ladda. We have the hall, the dock, and a dozen ships. Most here don't seem to care that we're here and Harald is gone."

"How long?" I ask.

"How long were you out? Half an hour? An hour, maybe. Enough for it to get dark."

"Help me up," I say, and he does, though it's clearly against his better judgment.

My head objects; there's a darkness and a pounding there.

The man is practically a giant, and he places my wincing shoulder over his, one hand on my hip. He could wear me like a scarf and not notice much, I think. He hands me my sword, and I thank him.

When we get to the door I tell him to put me down, and it's on unsteady feet that I enter the hall of Aalborg.

There are many dead, few wounded, so that all who hold this hall now, most into the mead, are in decent enough shape. They've had the sense to stay out of the great chair that has served, apparently, as a throne for the pretender-king Harald. Rorik's chair.

I have no such sense, and limp and drag my gory self to the seat of power. Someone hands me some wine. I almost put it down, the cup heavy and makes my shoulder complain, but I take it in for a moment. The oaken solidity of the chair, the pile of furs on it, the gold cup with Frankish wine. My crew, victorious and grateful, around the fire, flashing one another wounds, scars, and joking. The sound of their cheering as they raise their cups to me.

I'm sitting too, I realize, upon a cloak, rich and heavy. I put the cup down on the chair's table-sized arms, and carefully wrap myself up in the generous wool.

"Wake me when Ragnar gets here," I say, though I doubt anyone can hear me.

A dream.

I'm in my old dress, the one my mother made me. The one blood and war took from me that day on the beach. Only clean now. Mended.

Not mended. Perfect.

Everyone is gone. The world empty like the day I left the Gaular. There is a light the colour of sea-foam coming from outside the door of the hall of Aalborg, and I rise from the great chair without pain.

White steps in stone down to the water, which I know aren't really there, but still this path, under a moon, takes me to the shore.

A woman waits in a dress, now green, now blue, her hair shimmering copper. Her bare feet in the tide. A swan glides behind her, its black eyes watchful.

"*Meyla*," she says. "Come. Come sit."

"I am no longer a little girl, Skathi," I tell the goddess. "And there's nowhere to sit."

"As you wish," she says. "And no, no you're no longer a girl, Ladda."

"Why did you bring me here?" I ask her.

"You brought me," she says. "With you."

"You kept Harald's fleet to the north, so we could land on the southern shore," I say, trying to remember the day. It seems difficult.

"I did," says the goddess of tide. And of scars, I remember.

"What happens now?" I ask. Is that what this is about? Did I need to ask this?

"What would you wish for?" she asks.

"Same as always. I want to keep my people safe. Kara and Rota, safe."

"And you have done this," Skathi says.

"No. More," I tell her. "More than just for a year. I want them to have a life there, in the Gaular. With the great-aunts and the grey-beards and all the songs and memories and stories of my mother's people, my father's. I need..."

"Yes?" the goddess asks.

"I need my mother's runes to survive. The stories and secret of them. Kara's runes, now, and mine too, I suppose. I don't understand it yet. But that's why I have to go back. To learn them. To keep it safe. Alive. Remembered."

"You wish for silver, then," she states.

"Not silver, just what it can buy. A future. Survival."

"Silver," she says, nodding. And the sea sparkles with it, waves in moonlight. Fish scales. I can see dancing in their flash and play, forming individual runes.

Her runes are still spelling out the world. Runes of wealth, and transaction. Of the aurochs, great-shouldered cattle, and a thorn in a thicket, and the mouth of a god. And the god rides a chariot, its wheels spinning spokes which become a brand of fire. And the fire is a gift, then, in the darkness, warming hands and supper and becoming stories, all these hearth-side joys. And outside the hearth, a rain of hail, rattling and murmuring of need, of ice, and the wheel of the year, harvest long faded. And a yew tree, its wood now a dice cup spilling chance and fate, and an elk and the sun and a birch tree and..."

"Stop it," say. "Please. Stop. It's too much." I try not to look too apologetic. "All at once."

"You have a question," says the goddess, understanding, and she is once more one thing and not a thousand. The runes are still there in the glint of the waves, but less demanding.

"Should I marry Rorik?" This, I think, is the question I dragged to a goddess, or perhaps the other way around.

"Not for a palm of land," she answers cryptically.

"Does that mean no, or just not for his land?"

She says nothing. If Kara were here, I think, she could teach me how to make the gods more co-operative.

Behind the goddess, easing from the sea arises a great armada of ships. Dozens. Hundreds, maybe. More ships than in all the world. Karv and karr, skeith and buss, all of golden wood. Each fly a banner of a swan, wrought in knotwork. At the vanguard, a dragon-headed *drakkar*, one of the boats I took in victory over Harald as a prize.

As soon as it appears, the vision of the fleet subsides, and there is simply the lull of the ocean, and Skathi.

"Eindr thinks I'm the goddess Thorgertha," I tell her.

"I know," she says.

"Am I?" I ask.

"Are you?" Her voice is laughter, but it does not mock.

"Thorgertha's just a legend," I say.

"So are you, Ladda." says Skathi. "So are you."

And I'm awake.

"You're in my chair," Rorik says. He looks... normal. Untroubled. Composed. Certainly not fresh from battle.

"Where in all of Midgard were you?" I ask him, waking.

"North. We came overland, same as you. It just took a little longer"

"I hope you had a pleasant walk, Jarl Rorik," I say, pulling myself up to sitting straight. Shoulder and ribs complain, a wince and a gasp. My ear stings like a thousand wasps wage war against it, and I can't open one eye all the way.

"Not entirely uneventful. We did manage to persuade most of the households from staying out of the battle."

"What about joining our side?" I ask.

"There's only so much one can expect," he replies.

"Ragnar?" I ask.

"At the docks, drinking. He should be here any minute. A great feast is upon us, if we can get the kitchen fires hot enough so late. But I think it'll be worth their while."

"I'm in no mood for a feast," I tell him, though I'm suddenly starving at the thought of food.

"I need to get my ships," I finish.

"At dawn we'll send horses, enough crew to bring them to dock here, though we're running out of room," he chuckles.

"And the fleet?"

"Few losses," he assures me. "None of mine or yours as far as I can tell. Some of Ragnar's. Still, there are sixty boats in the harbour."

"Sixty!" We have again doubled a fleet we've opposed. One final question. "And Harald?"

"Escaped. Or it seems so. Some of his fleet broke off late in the battle and headed south. Ragnar wanted to pursue but didn't have the numbers. Still, Harald is broken after this. He borrowed a great deal of silver to pay for the ships now under our control. And most of the jarls will support Ragnar now that he's back in the Jutland."

"So, it's over," I say.

"War is business, Ladda," he says, touching my sliced ear gingerly. "It is never over."

We have had to wait until Friday for the wedding. The day of Freja, goddess of love.

A great deal was made over whether to do it here, or move on in a show of force to Viborg for a more public display. Ragnar, in his fickle way, decided to remain in Aalborg, which has been doubling in population every hour throughout the week as householders stream in to prove their loyalty. And, of course, to distance themselves from Harald, whom they all claim to despise. Politics.

Thora for her part is beautiful, and there's an expectation that I will somehow find myself in her wake like the other prominent women of Aalborg. But I don't know how to set my hair or how I'm to wear the dresses here. Ragnar solves this problem by sending two girls to the house Rorik has lent me, and they simply dress me like a doll as I stand there.

Last night there was a great blot, which while it was expected of me to go, I was forgiven in my absence to recover from my injuries. Although despite an angry red line on my ear, with a bit missing no more than the nip of a mouse, and the great bruise on my cheek, both are largely unseen. My shoulder has made simple things such as brushing my hair impossible, and my ribs ache when I sit too long, or stand too long, or sleep more than an hour.

But also, there's a hardness to my words, to my voice, to my dreams.

In battle, in the midst of blows exchanged, there's no room for fear. Or if it was there it was polite enough to wait its turn and not demand my attention. But at night it comes, and I wake with my heart in my throat and my hands trembling. I hear the bones against my shield, smell the blood's metal hit the air, and the stink of the offal on a withdrawn spear. It's not the roaring during, but the screaming after. The whimpering and mewling, the twisted songs of pain. This is what haunts me. And I wear it as much as I wear this grand dress Ragnar has sent me for his wedding.

A wedding that could have been mine.

I'm surprised this doesn't bother me. Should it? But no, Thora is beautiful and I suppose that it's her purpose to be beautiful. I was more jealous (was I jealous?) to see them flirt. But all these details of *mundr,* the bride-price and the morning-gift of *morgengifu* just look like the hall-dealings of port access and bails of wool. It's just business. Rorik would agree.

I've begun to notice the way he looks at me, battered creature though I am. Eyeing me up like a horse he considers buying. Maybe I should see him the same way. Business.

Even then, there is a glint there. We intrigue each other. Could we be lovers? I don't entirely trust him, but then I doubt he would want me to. He's a complicated thing. So different from Ragnar, whose nature assumed I would share my bed and it was easy as yawning. Much laughter back then, hoping not to be heard by all who no doubt heard us. Maybe I miss that. Maybe that's why I resent Thora, to what little extent I do, or might.

But it was the fear that made me excuse myself from the blot. I've seen enough animal-dread in the eyes of the people I've killed; I have no pressing need to see the same fear in the faces of animals facing sickle or rope, left hanging in the forest like Odinn from Yggdrasil, the Tree of Worlds. Is the god so satisfied, that his own suffering is reflected back to him in offering? I have only met one god, so I couldn't know. Maybe Kara has met Odinn. Maybe she's wed to him by now, there is no telling with my god-bound sister, whom I miss painfully, and such missing is a fist of ice in my chest.

However, there is a wedding to endure. At the end of which I shall return to the Gaulardale with at least twenty ships and near eight hundred crew, stopping along the Jutland to collect families, livestock, household goods, and I mean to create a great village that will be defended, peopled, and enduring. A future I've purchased with my sword and my nightmares.

One wedding to endure.

Ragnar seems happy, and he embraced me when it was over. His great arms around me and he lifts me just a little off the ground (which makes my shoulder crunch in a hideous way), because he can. Not the embrace of a former lover, but of a comrade. I do see now that I love him, although not in a way either of us could have expected.

Thora kissed me on the cheek as I gave her the blessing I could remember, words of my mother's which seemed odd in my mouth, but they were received well. She's my queen now, I suppose, a contract.

"Jarl Hladgertha, a word?" Turning, it's Eindr, his face expressionless.

"Of course, Eindr," I smile, hoping he'll smile back. And he does, just a little, though this pleases me more than it should. We walk together away from the throng of well-wishers, all crowned with flowers and some already into the ale.

"Jarl Rorik would like to know what you plan to do," he says.

"Don't you?" I ask.

"Me?" He's puzzled.

"You're not curious?"

I've led him between granaries, the wood silver in the sun, sanded soft from seasons, yet it catches on the sleeve of my dress. Not for long, not a snag, just the plucking at a thread. A place for private conversations, or stolen ones.

"Well," he says, relaxing, less formal. "I imagine you'll do what you said you'd do. Take your ships and your silver and go back to your village to build."

I nod.

"But Rorik has an offer," I say.

"He does, Ladda," Eindr says carefully.

"I've been expecting as much." I'm trying to look unconcerned, but it's not working. I keep looking at the shape of his face.

"Jarl Rorik would marry you. He would grant you a large bride-price of lands in Aalborg that would bring in an annual fee, allowing you to garrison your village with two hundred men and their families."

"I have eight hundred crew," I insist.

"Yes, but you'll need to feed them. And almost all are Jutlanders which will not want to remain so far north."

"It's not so bad in the Nordvegr," I say. "At least in the Vestfold." I can't imagine them not wanting to come. The Gualar is green, and quiet.

"It's warmer here," he says. "With more grazing land. Ladda, if you dropped eight hundred people in your village it would be like an invasion."

He's right, of course. There would be more Danes than any of my village have ever seen, and their ways, their stories, would swallow ours in a generation.

"Two hundred," Eindr continues, "year after year, that gives you strength with fewer mouths for the land to feed."

"We have salmon," I retort.

"Eight hundred people require a great deal of salmon," he says. "Or so Rorik would tell you, I'm sure."

"I'm sure," I say. He's still right. And I've thought about this, night after night, staving off dark dreams by untangling this knot, and I've known it. I didn't like the taste of the fact in my throat.

"So Jarl Rorik would have you stay. Send five boats with those who would go, leave the rest of the fleet here in Aalborg. And you, too, would remain with him."

There's a weight on me. I can feel it pressing my shoulders down to the earth, my heart sinking to my belly.

"Eindr," I say, "what do you think I should do?"

He pauses, considering. "For my part, Ladda, I would see you happy."

"Happy?" I'm not even sure what that means anymore.

"Yes. I think you deserve happiness." His honesty and kindness are chipping away months of hardness from me, and I'm not sure I want that. Not now.

"Can I be happy here, with Rorik?" I ask. Would he even know?

"I can't tell you that, Ladda." and I notice when he drops the title, that he has for most of this conversation. "But I do hope you could be happy here." He smiles, too briefly, then clearly fearing he's crossed some line, stiffens and steps back.

I've been standing too long, and everything is beginning to throb again.

"I need to rest," I say. "But tell Rorik..." What? Tell him what a goddess told me in a dream? The pause makes me look like an idiot.

"Jarl Hladgertha?" Eindr asks, again formal, concerned.

"Tell him I will agree to marry him, but not for one palm of his land."

"Then what would you like?" he asks. All business.

"The fleet," I say, remembering the vision of a forest of masts, all under the banner of a swan. "The ships are to be mine. All of them."

"All of them," he repeats, nodding, dismissing himself courteously.

And Eindr is gone and I'm leaning against the grain shed, my palm pressed into its sun-silvered wood, trying not to throw up.

Unsuccessfully, it turns out.

— PART III —

I wake in my bed with no sign of my husband. There are a few candidates for whose bed I might find him in, but I don't care to look for him. It's an insult, and it's likely meant to be.

The winter has been the easiest of my life. I have no chores, no worry. There's always meat, and bread. There are hands to tend the fires and hands to pour Rorik wine. Always more wine. And sometimes his own hand reaches out to those who welcome the touch of a gold-ringed hand.

Wife. I taste the word with my tongue, roll it around in my mouth.

I've shared my bed with two men; a king and a jarl. The king was always a thing of hunger, boy-like in the way boys throw themselves naked off the dock in summer. Joyous and wild, then ravenous, always laughing. But sometimes impatient, ungentle. With Ragnar it was the strength of his arms and his legs, the desperation in his mouth, like swimming. Like drowning.

But my husband, Rorik—he's an articulate lover. Fingertips, lips, the hair brushed gently from my face, his kisses on my throat, between my breasts, down my belly. A tongue-tip skillfully flicked on a hip-bone. An attention artful, cultivated. But it's been months without, and I sleep alone or for warmth in a pile of the girls who braid my hair.

Caldr returned not long after Ragnar left with his queen to his halls in Heithabyr. Throughout these months Rorik's table has been haunted by Caldr and his grumbling, an unprofitable war in the north against lands once loyal to Fro. I can tell him that many of the villages he's raided had never heard of their supposed king, or of his war against Siward and Ragnar, but no word of mine has any weight at all in his ears, and increasingly I'm waved away by the man I married, the man whose fate my own is now tied by troth. By contract.

As the month of Thorri fades into Goi, ice recedes from the harbour, and the men speak more of war. And Rorik speaks of war as though the ships frozen to the dock for another month or so are not mine, their crews promised to me as bride-price.

Months since word from the Gaular. The voice of Brandr echoed in the messenger, sailing south, who tells me the garrison is established, as is trade with the village upriver Ragnar and I discovered. Rota and Kara are well, Kara unchallenged in her role as jarl in my place. And this is all I know of what I've left behind.

Safe, in a single word. If only this were enough to allow me to breathe all the way in and all the way out, just once. I thought it would be. I thought it should be.

I have spent the months of Ylir and Morsugur shaking off my attendants, with their combs and trenches, and training with my crew in the snow. My shoulder healed, it's supple again, and stronger now with a spear. My sword however is wrapped in goatskin and tucked away in a box near my bed, and I fear picking it up; I fear what it cost me, fear that I've shamed it by what I've become.

And what is that? Kept and ignored? Surely that's not all I am. I've made good on my word so that the Gaular would not fall to wolf or winter. So that's something. The rest is merely the idleness of the first snow I've never been required to brave in search of firewood or rabbits. Is there guilt in that? Some, if I'm honest with myself.

I can see why Rorik finds solace in Frankish wine and admiring girls. He tries to erase the cost of sitting on a fur-piled throne, cup in hand, while others work and freeze. It's too much to face entirely sober.

Mercifully, few expect sons to begin issuing from me like eggs from a hen this year. Not yet. Of course, I'd need my husband to share my bed for this to happen, and then with more blood than wine in his veins.

I think he's a different man in summer months. The Rorik I know–kind, clever, knowledgeable about the world–will return with the sun. But each night Caldr is there at the table like a storm cloud, blocking out any hint of sunrise.

I shake my head of the whole thing. Rising, the girls who attend me today fetch cloak and basin. I nod for my wolf skin, still a collar due to my mother's brooch. I no longer bow my head to allow them to slip it on, as I expect them to manage. They can get a box, if they have to.

I should learn their names. But I'm afraid that every face, every meal, every morning tethers me to this place and not to my own home, my own people, where I'm jarl in my own right.

I want the cold air on my face. Winter is honest, at least. It promises nothing other than that which it brings. Mud and dung from the pens are smoothed over, ripe scents stifled, sound turned to whispers. The creak of the ice is that of the pines in the wind.

So I stand just outside the door of my house until my cheeks hurt, and my eyes slit against the sun on the snow.

Eindr slides the white game piece across the board, smiling.

When we play he insists always that I am to be red—outnumbered and surrounded, avoiding capture. I have enough of that away from the board.

I always thought *tafl* was a game for old men, but Eindr says it's designed to teach strategy. So in each game we pretend the king-piece is me ashore, surrounded by my crew and cut off from our boats. The enemy is white, in the forest, four separate forces trying to coordinate and pen us in before we can reach the river, which is the table's edge. We feint, plan, fall back, counter.

I have my own weapons at my disposal, despite the fact that the king-piece cannot capture enemy forces.

If my eyes catch his, he looks away, swallowing, and his hands unsteady after. When it's my move I look off for a moment, play with my hair or adjust the rings on my fingers until I feel him watching me. He doesn't let me win, but I can distract him, evade.

And so we pass the hours, and with each dawn the crack of ice sloughing off the harbour is a day closer to my escape.

"I plan on leaving, you know," I tell him, as though it were nothing. I move a game piece, closing ranks.

"I know," he admits.

"And?"

"And what?" he says, almost laughing.

"What does my husband think of this?"

"Jarl Rorik's thoughts are his own, Jarl Hladgertha." I never know when he's teasing me with my title and formal name.

"Eindr, you know him better than anyone," I press.

"I don't believe that's true," he says, sliding a white piece across the board. An obvious move.

"Regardless, what do you think he thinks?" I could crack open my friend's skull sometimes, he's so elusive.

Eindr's response is careful.

"You own the fleet, but not the crew. Jarl Rorik can't allow you to leave Aalborg without ships, and there's no profit in allowing some three hundred warriors to leave with you simply because you wish to visit your family."

"So?" I had assumed as much. I slide a counter piece, making slow progress.

"So whatever you offer to pay them to leave, he will pay them more to stay." His fingers hover above a game piece, contemplating.

"A bidding war," I say.

"One you can't win. Ships without crew are wood, crew without ships are farmers. And little profit is found in trading the axe for the plough."

"A draw, then," I suggest.

"Certainly a position with which to begin negotiations," he says, pretending that this is all theory.

"So, in this scenario, what should I negotiate for?"

He moves before speaking. Then: "A single ship, to Hjorring."

"And why Hjorring?" I ask, though I think I know.

"Early spring trade, gather news. Harald is still out there, somewhere, and you can rule out the north as a scout. No open ocean, easy to beach if a storm hits on the way. No risk, and a chance of reward if you hear of anything. Many here have family there, and will even pay for the passage. Offset your cost."

"And from there..." I say, sliding a red piece in defense.

"Well, at that point you are a day's sail south of the Nordvegr, with a paid crew under your command, and Jarl Rorik nowhere in sight. Where you sail after that is entirely your concern."

His last white move falls short of my defences, and I slide my king piece to a corner. Escape.

Victory.

"Something suitable then," I say. "The drakkar."

The dragon-headed boat of war. My prize.

———◄●►———

When the storm hits, it's at least predictable. I'm getting bored of cursing myself.

Hjorring was uneventful. Business was conducted, families reunited, there were gifts of courtesy and diplomacy. Rorik has a trade-house there, to store whatever balance or profit is left over from such dealings, and I mean to gather it all on the return journey.

If we survive.

The storm is leaden and growls like an animal. A sea black with white teeth.

We row, all of us, every hand, and I lend my back to the oars, pulling just so we can stay in place, to be hammered again and again by the freezing rain. The alternative is to be dragged west, out to sea, our only hope then to snag some island—if there is one—before being swamped and drowned.

Lightning catches the ring on my finger. A purple glass bead set in silver, and a line in Arabic I can't read. Eindr gave it to me when I left, as it was mine anyway, he said. Rorik had no interest in the thing.

"What does it say?" I had asked Eindr.

"It is the name of the Arabic god," he explained.

"Just the one?"

"Their god is vast. It contains all the qualities of all the gods."

"So much," I said in awe. And I thought how our gods are in turn temperamental, foolish, selfish, yet intimately loving. Human, though grander and more fickle. So in this way, we're their children. A god with so many faces, all at once, seems a cold and distant being, and I can't pretend to understand it.

It's Thor now who tests us. Not some distant god of all but a presence here, now, sudden and violent, throwing light and fire at us. The Skagerrak Sea at the end of winter is still a dice cup, and we'll see what comes out of it. We row until we're nearly dead.

But nearly dead is still alive, and to cease rowing is to cease breathing air.

Hour, and an hour, and an hour, hands blistered, backs burning, eyes blinded by salt and wind, each beam and rivet aching for release like a bowstring pulled back and back and back.

But the dragon-head is fearsome itself, and we're not so easily swept aside by the whim of a god. Our boat gains distance, oar-stroke by oar-stroke, one cursed breath at a time, until the storm subsides into a spitting thing the colour of wet wool, spent of malice, still rich in misery.

And so, a fire is set in the tripod, and we warm frozen fingers and dig out layers unsodden from the thwarts. Some are lucky enough to find something dry.

Two lost. Two men whose name I never knew are simply gone from a crew of forty. Somehow plucked away from those sitting next to them without noticing. Words and prayers are uttered, and mead is poured overboard in memory. Some will mourn later. Most will forget. But there is meat, and fire, and rest for now, even some shelter beneath leather tents.

Every wound I ever took is howling now: a broken finger, my ribs, my shoulder, even the crack in my cheek which has yet to heal all the way and may never, all a chorus of throbbing reminders. We're all held together with scars, and that barely.

The tide is pulling us east now, the sails down as the wind from the north does us no favours. Hopefully not so far east as to land us in the Svear, but we'll see.

Thor has let us go, and Skathi, lady of tides, has us now.

The stone in the water nearly makes me burst into tears.

A large, round stone in the midst of the river, which is at least full as the snow has given the first hint of melting.

I'm thinking of the last time I saw it, with Rota beside me, remembering the summers we spent as naked and swimming children, trying to catch salmon with our bare hands and failing, laughing. And then seeing it as a signpost of my uncle's lodge, our journey from massacre and captivity to some kind of weary hope, my wolf skin new and raw over my shoulders.

I could have taken the longer route, past the fjord and inland from the river to the north. The route Ragnar came to claim me. But whether it was impatience or faith in the draw of my boat, we took the shorter path, though the oars scrape the river bed here in parts.

What I was expecting was... not this. What I left, maybe, only stronger. More huts with grass roofs. A new barn or granary. But not this.

The river's been dredged here to make way for a port the size of Aalborg, with three docks jutting out into the river in a curve, and these are ringed by a stone wall. There's a girl with a crown of winterflowers in her hair and a good woolen cloak who sees us and runs; she's the bearer of news. But I can hear the town, the lowing of cattle, a blacksmith's hammer somewhere. And all this behind the fleet of my dreams.

Gods, there must be thirty ships here.

By the time we reach the dock there are horns sounded, and bells, and cheering. I make out familiar faces in what seems like a sea of unfamiliar ones. There's no sign of Rota. No sign of Kara.

But there is Brandr, standing proudly, if leaning a bit on his spear.

As we dock and lines are thrown, I can see into the new boats. Wet from winter, but the wood still new and golden, curves unworn from hand or storm or battle. Each a field of snow without so much as a single footprint.

Hands reach out to me, generous smiles, horns of ale thrust at me and a thousand questions of war, trade, weather, families. It's a beautiful madness. A boy scurries past, chased laughing by others. Villi, the boy I saved from the wolf, grown a head taller by a single winter.

And then I come to Brandr, who smiles to the point of a tear on his cheek, and he embraces me near to smothering. I hold him as though all the scents of home could be pressed into my heart like this, and there is the memory of the fragrance of my father, sweat and smoke.

He lets go, though his hands never leave my shoulders.

"Jarl Hladgertha, welcome home."

"Gods, Brandr, what have you done?" I ask in astonishment, looking past his shoulder at the village.

"What you have done. What your silver has brought us. Walk with me, and I'll take you to your sister."

I have smiles and thanks to return to the crowd, which seems reluctant to make room for our progress to the hall.

Brandr continues. "Ragnar's troops gave us a good start, but it was Rorik's people who got us ahead of the winter. We had a good harvest, with plentiful fish. Everything else we traded with Vikoryi."

"The town upriver," I nod, putting it together, though I've never heard the name.

"Yes, they turned out to be excellent neighbours once they realized we were fortified and convinced we would neither attack nor leave. There are some families which have homesteaded half-way, and they've done well enough. But come. How was the journey?"

"We lost two," I tell him. "A storm in the Skagerrak."

"A terrible thing," he says gravely.

The path from the docks to the hall is paved with flat stones, quarried from somewhere not conveniently near. There is the constant scratch of sweeping. So many houses, and not just dug into the earth but erected with great beams and clad in planks. Cooking smells I don't recognize.

I enter a hall, and it takes a moment to realize that it is in fact my hall. The floor now boarded and covered in hide. The old boat-shaped hearth still there, but further towards the back a great trench of stone with split wood stacked all around. And behind that, a chair I'd never seen before, piled with furs, and upon them, my little slip of a sister, pale and beautiful.

"Kara!" and I rush to her, nearly pulling her off the chair as her arms are around me as when we were girls, when I'd carry her over brambles or carry her back to my mother after a scraped knee or bee sting. Her hair smells like smoke, but also like honey and some flower I can't identify. I press her into the Kara-shaped hole in my heart, and am amazed she still fits. After everything.

"Hladgertha," she says. "I knew you were coming today."

"Who told you?" I ask, teasing. "Elves or gods?"

"Runes."

"Of course," I say. I pull her away. "Let me look at you, Jarl Kara."

"I'm not the jarl," she says. "You are." She's grown. Taller and more beautiful, a hint of our mother about her that's stronger now. But there's also a confidence, and a presence in the world—this world—that's new.

"This chair suits you," I tell her.

"I missed you, Ladda," she says, a child again. "I missed you so much."

"Where is Rota?" I ask.

"Rota kept your promise," Kara says. "A harvest and a winter. And now is off to war."

"To war? What war?" And my heart is suddenly pounding at the prospect that I've left my people in danger.

"Raiding. Some of the warriors are raiding the villages that supported Fro last year." I think of Caldr's unsuccessful raids against the Svear, and wonder if Rota is mixed up in all that somehow.

"And what do the runes say about Rota?" I ask, not really believing.

"Rota is dead, I think," Kara tells me. It's as though she is discussing the weather.

The air is out of me. There is nothing I can say to this, and no breath to say it with. This can't be right. It can't be.

"No. What?"

"I haven't heard anything, I just think so," Kara says. I breathe deeply, like being deep underwater and then breaking to the surface.

"Well then, let's keep Rota among the living until the runes or the elves tell you otherwise, all right?" and she nods at this in agreement, seeming somewhat relieved.

"You've seen her," Kara says definitively, and I know at once what she means.

The goddess.

"Yes. In…in a dream. And once as a swan, I think."

She just nods. It's all she wanted. "You're married now," she continues. "We heard."

"Jarl Rorik, yes." There's an edge to my voice I haven't intended.

"Do you love him?" she asks. A simple question a girl asks of an older sister, though I look around before I answer.

"He's a good man," I say, the answer to a different question.

"Is he?" And this, a third question.

"I hope so."

"But you're not happy," she says. "Not like Brown-eyes."

"What?" I ask, though I know. I just don't know how she knows.

"Brown-eyes. He makes you happy."

"He does," I say, and tears are coming to my eyes though I don't know why. "But he's my friend."

"Your husband will kill your friend," warns Kara, suddenly from a distance, "but only if he knows."

I take both of Kara's hands in mine.

"I wish that I could take this off you, all the things you know." I let go of a hand and wipe my cheeks, sniff in a way my mother would have scolded me for.

"Here. I brought you gifts," I say, remembering. "They're on the ship. Dresses and beads. Things for the house."

"I don't care about that stuff," says Kara. "I'm just glad you're back for good."

"Am I?" I ask, honestly.

"Aren't you?"

"I hope so, Kara. I hope so."

There's less business than I thought. Kara wanted a blot before any councils were held, but I overruled her. The gods have taken enough of a price from me. Let some goat bleat for another day.

Kara's judgments were both rare and just, Brandr's council wise and in the interest of peace. That the people of Vikoryi would trade rather than simply take speaks well of the land, and the choice we made coming here. The hungry are rarely so agreeable.

But still, I lean heavily on Brandr for advice, and wish to all the gods that I had persuaded Rorik to allow me to bring Eindr. This, now that I think of it, is the first time in days I've remembered my husband at all, but Eindr, my friend and tafl-opponent, is rarely out of my head. And there's a weight on my chest when I think about him... it's best not to think about him.

There have been feuds. Not between villages, but among Ragnar's warriors. There were blows, and suit was brought to Kara. Brandr says he felt that sides were being divided, so once he had the promise that peace would be kept by both arguing parties, he speared one through the back in the hall. As some drew weapons in outrage, he persuaded all there of the wisdom of his actions, and that seemed to be the end of it.

In the early days after I left there were disputes and agreements that led to some householders owning three-fifths of a cow, but this became something of a running joke. A family from Vikoryi sought to contract one ten-year-old girl from the Gaular in troth to their son, but Kara forbade it, at least for five years, and this too was taken well and with patience. So, too, was her decision, despite the protests of some farmers, that a particular stone of elvish interest was not to be moved, and in the end, they ploughed around it.

So, with the security of food and person assured, the entire village threw itself into what they understood was my wish—boatbuilding. Almost all have had their first sea trials within the last few weeks, with the river at last clear of all ice, and the more experienced of Ragnar's crew have been recruiting and training the bored and aspiring sons of Vikoryi. So there's almost, but not quite, enough hands to crew the fleet here.

Contracts have to be made to secure enough iron for rivets and shield bosses, which I have learned is different from the iron used in pots and hinges. There's a source, but the traders want some kind of long-term interest in the land, which I'll have to think about. Still, there are forty shields needed for each boat, and currently a hole in the center of each shield. The blacksmith, Brandr assures me, can work the iron once it arrives, after a deal is made.

I have brought not only gifts for Kara (and Rota, which will have to wait) but also adornments from Hjorring, so that doorways and the end caps of tables can be chased with silver and bronze beasts, in knotwork. A year ago, I would have thought of this as a waste of metal, but now I see that it adds stability to a place, and is a kind of blessing.

There are those here who now seek to return south, their service to Ragnar having been completed, and will need boats for that. Some will stay, and that too is a blessing. When Brandr asks of my plans, I think only of sleep, so later as I climb into bed with Kara as we did when we were small, and she my wild and tiny sister-thing with the whistling snores of a barn cat, I think I should miss Rota more.

Though the eyes I think of as I fall asleep are not Rota's, but Eindr's.

Weeks of this, and it's dreamlike.

Snows recede like all the storms were some bad dream, the aches in me from fetching wood or helping my mother in the kitchen. But the mornings I wake up cold, barely breathing, the faces of pain and fear filling my vision. Men whose death I brought. There's a bruise inside me, or a gutting, that doesn't show, though sometimes I see a similar wound in the eyes of others before we both look away.

Nights, Kara tells me the stories of the runes, to see as she sees. Not just sounds scratched in wood, but more like the stories of ancient families, with conflict and love, of friction and ease. About how the first sound in a line can recall an entire saga, just by placing it ever so slightly towards or away from the next. Still, to me, most of these are coded references to stories I've never heard.

"You need to teach others," I say. "This is too important."

She just shakes her head.

I'm no *skald*, no story-keeper. I never will be. I'm grateful to learn this as best as I'm able, but it's almost like my heart is too small to bear a secret this big.

No, it's not that. My heart is large enough. It's just that the stories themselves don't wish to live there. I can feel them tapping on the inside of my chest, like we're doing something wrong. Though not when Kara tells them. It fits for her.

I don't know.

For the most part, as flowers return and some sense of normalcy asserts itself, it's easy to forget, even for an hour at a time. Those returning south were making plans, packing, set on delivering those boats Ragnar had already paid for.

"So much livestock," I mention to Brandr, noticing the rattle and bleat of them as Brandr and I walk the path to the docks.

"We agreed," he says. "No slaughter last year. The meat we bought from Vikoryi, and we went sealing in the fall."

"Still, the numbers." I'm impressed.

"Oh, these are ours," he says smiling. "Shortly after you left I sent a party of Ragnar's men to the coast, to the old village site. They came back a week later with cows, sheep, goats. Even horses."

I'm stunned at this.

"How?"

"During the raid," Brandr tells me, "most just opened the pens. The raiders took most of the horses, yes, but the livestock scattered to the hills, and we didn't get the chance to collect many of them. Over time they drifted back to the village."

"And what of the remainders?" I remember that I had declared they would be left with nothing.

"There were a few, they said. Perhaps a dozen living in the ruins. Some complained, but Ragnar's men were armed, on horseback. They were told they could return with the men to the Gaulardale, or they could stay and catch fish all winter."

"But none returned."

"None, Ladda."

Mine were always a stubborn people. They had expected to die there, that night, and their extra months of life were more burden than boon.

Brandr and I often stroll now as we discuss the business of the town. How to get goods to the markets of Kaupang without paying Vikoryi as a go-between, how much silver we're likely to get from Ragnar for the other boats, or if there is a market for them which doesn't require crossing the Skagerrak. I realize now that I've spent more time in this village— the one with stone walls and its bustling dock—than I did the one I left behind, the village of refugees staring into a distant yet menacing winter. I'm glad of it.

And then the bell robs me of all gladness.

Instinct has me reaching for shield and spear I'm not carrying; that I'm nowhere near. I stride toward the hall with more fire in my veins than the ice which first cascaded through them.

I see Kara there and shoot her a look.

"No warning from your elf friends?" I fire at her, but she is in some kind of shock, and I feel bad for saying it.

In a linden-wood box by my bed is my sword. Someone brings me a shield and a spear.

By the time I leave the hall's threshold, perhaps a hundred heartbeats since I entered it, my fear has calmed somewhat. A corridor of warriors, fifty a side, greet me with shield and helm, spearpoints glinting in the spring sun. There are twenty men on horseback, the horses pacing backwards with their blood up.

Wolf's-heads. Or the upriver town of Vikoryi, come to take whatever they wish. Raiders from what remains of Fro's forces after the war looking for retribution for their defeat. Whichever, we stand armed.

Trained. Experienced.

Ready.

"Horses," I say, and those mounted bolt into the forest path in the north, the same path where I met Ragnar a year ago.

A year ago, when I was barely sixteen and had only killed two men and a wolf.

I won't go with the horses, but will stay and fight in the shield wall if it comes to it. We wait for a rider to return, and will set up positions once we know what we're fighting.

Brandr remains with me, even though I've dismissed him and told him to go with the guards who've taken Kara to a boat for safety.

"I would not want you to die today, Brandr," I tell him.

"I'm reluctant to do so myself," he says. "Let's see what news from the rider, eh? Maybe I'll die tomorrow."

And we wait for an hour.

None dare put down their shields, though five pounds of wood and iron seems like fifty after a few minutes. The butts of spears begin to rest in the earth. The bell has stopped, and each ear strains for the sound of tack and horse, or the snap and crunch of a marching horde. Nothing but the breeze and songbirds. For an hour.

A mistake, the bell, I think. We're all thinking it. No smoke for fire. Perhaps some child who—

And then the unmistakable cadence of hoofbeats. A rider at last.

"It's the king!" shouts the man, rasping from the ride and sending spittle in his beard. "It's Ragnar!"

What has Hel coughed up on my apron? Ragnar?

Sighs of relief, even stifled cheers, emerge from my forces. There is some laughter as the tension fades and the pounding of comrades' shoulders.

Ragnar.

Here he comes, with all my riders in tow and commingled with his own. Horns passed horse to horse, all brothers reunited.

I could cheerfully spear the lot of them.

"I'm all out of dogs for you to kill, Goat Pants," I call to him, displeased.

Smiling, he rides right up to me, saying nothing before he dismounts.

"Is that any way to greet an old friend?" he grins. The light catches in the blonde of his beard.

"You are looking old," I tell him. "Marriage disagrees with you."

"Winter was unkind," he says. "To me at least. You, however, look as beautiful as the day I met you."

"Flatterer," I say. "I looked like a mess the day you met me."

"I'm thirsty, Ladda. Find us a drink, a place to speak."

I look around at the bustle of the town, intrigued by new faces, new stories, new flirtations.

"It looks like a feast is happening regardless," I say. "Well, come on in then." I turn to the hall without seeing if Ragnar will follow.

I cross the hall and take my chair, even though custom says I should yield it to him. He seems untroubled by this and drags a stool over.

"I missed you at Aalborg," he says.

"When were you at Aalborg?"

"No, I mean I arrived just after you left. Are you really reluctant to see me?" He seems hurt.

"No, of course not. It's just... I don't know. Like I've been living a kind of fantasy here. A dream." The hall is coming to life, with casks creaking open and wooden trenchers clacking on the tables. Firewood clatters beside the hearth as boys argue about how to stoke the fire.

"And I woke you." His blue eyes are flashing in the light.

"You're trouble," I agree, half-smiling.

"That's why you like me."

"Who says I like you?"

"You have to like me. You're my best friend." And I look at the blue of his eyes and the scars on his hands, remember how happy he was at his wedding feast and how his happiness moved my own, and yes, I suppose I am his best friend.

There's a crackle of cedar on the hearth, and the scent of it reminds me of fires past, and hours with the man in front me. which brings me to the moment.

"All right, but what about Thora?" I ask. "Where is she?"

"She is my wife. She's where she's supposed to be, in my hall at Heithabyr."

"Being queen," I add.

"Being queen," he agrees.

"So you are here because?" A woman hands us both cups of water, with an assurance of wine or ale coming, and then disappears.

"Because you are not where you are supposed to be," says Ragnar, "but here instead. So here I am as well."

"You're as cryptic as my sister's elves," I tell him. "You want something."

"Need," he says, taking a bite of an apple handed to him.

"You need boats? We were about to deliver them."

"I heard! And more, too, I hear."

"We've been busy," I say.

"Ladda," Ragnar says, suddenly serious, or at least serious for Ragnar, "Harald is back."

"He survived the battle at Aalborg," I conclude.

"He did. And he barely let the ice melt before making trouble. He wintered in Sjeland, where they have no love for him. But now he's back in Jutland, and he has rallied the towns between Heithabyr and Aalborg. Even Viborg will side with him in this war."

I'm shocked by this.

"How could Viborg fall so easily?"

"It hasn't. Not yet. But he's paying families to stand aside, and I think they might."

"What about loyalty?" I'm furious. After what I've fought for, I have a right to be.

"Oh, many will fight for me, when it comes to it. I'm hoping it won't."

I sip before speaking.

"I can't help, Ragnar. I lost two men just getting here. And when your garrison leaves with you, it will be a month at least before troops arrive from Aalborg." There is a long pause while I listen to him chew. "I'm sorry."

"Rorik says you abandoned his bed," Ragnar says carefully.

I almost snort. "I'm surprised he could find his bed, with so much wine in him."

"I went there looking for you, as I said. Aalborg, not his bed." He grins at this last bit. "He says if you will not be wife to him, he will not send a garrison."

"You're just saying that. I don't believe you." I can't let myself.

"He says he's bound to let you keep the ships, in name only, but there is no law which compels him to defend the Nordvegr, particularly when there's no war here and nothing to defend it from." Again, a bite of the apple. "No profit in it, he says."

"He gave me his word," I say, seething.

"You should have had a contract," he says reluctantly. "Eindr is good at this sort of thing. You should use him."

"I did. We have a contract," I snap. "Is the word of my husband worth nothing?" I'm beyond angry. Shaking. "This is Caldr's doing."

He nods, agreeing. "Likely. Caldr's a pig. But if you would return to Aalborg, Rorik would have no choice but to honour your agreement."

I have nowhere to go with all this breath I'm holding. A sigh will have to do.

"Clearly you didn't come all this way to tell me this, Ragnar."

"I need your help, I told you." He chews with his mouth open, but tries to cover this with his fingers, like a little boy.

"But I can't..." I protest.

"We both know what you are going to do," he says.

"Oh, we do, do we?" I'm too tired to pursue this now.

"Your runes," he says. "The runes here. They are different, yes?"

I pause. How much does he know? How much should he know? I've shared it with him, but it seems like a lifetime ago, and I've learned so much more since then.

"Yes," I answer finally.

"So, you have come back, to this place, to protect them," he concludes.

"They're not just sounds to us. They're stories. Old stories. They're part of why we have to survive. Why we fled here in the first place, though I didn't realize it at the time."

"So you would see them survive," he says.

"Yes," I repeat.

"Then they can survive here, in this little valley, tucked away in the Nordvegr, or your stories, your runes, can take root in the wider world. More skalds, out there," he says, waving generally toward the door. "Find them. Teach them."

I have to think on this, and my face shows it.

"And that," Ragnar says, "is how we know what you'll do next."

"You said that." I'm smiling again. He's teasing me, at first, but then his tone is serious, or as serious as Ragnar gets.

"You are who you are. Rorik is not a man of his word, but you are a woman of yours. So you're going to come with me to Aalborg, and you'll force Rorik to garrison your town here. Then, because you are very, very good at what you do, you will come with me and we will kill Harald." One last bite of the apple.

"Together."

The goat did not bleat for long. The arrival and swift departure of a king demanded more sacrifice, and the black earth was glad of it. Or so Kara says.

"I will return as soon as I can," I tell Kara, near-smothering her into my cloak.

"Almost," she says.

"What does that mean?"

"Almost as soon as you can." She seems untroubled by this, but it makes no sense to me.

I kiss her forehead, and tuck her hair behind her ears. I have nothing to carry as I mount my horse.

We leave by the northern path, almost a road now, to the river and Ragnar's ships. The Gualar-fleet of near thirty will meet us at the mouth of the fjord, though some will have to be towed.

I miss Rota, miss that strength, in a way that makes my bones ache. In another life, my life of a year ago, I would be near-sobbing in Brandr's arms begging him to take care of everything, but now a year is past and I no longer need to beg. I never did, I know now.

Still, Kara is too young to be jarl in her own right and Brandr too old, even if he were willing. So I remain the jarl of the Gaular, even as I abandon it again in the first days of the month of Harpa.

To the south then. To war.

We meet the fleet, Ragnar's fleet, I suppose—they're his boats after all—timbers so new they're practically green, just north of the Sognefjord, where the islands are broken and jagged. So many of my people lie here, their breath taken by the sea and their bones shattered on the rocks. I pray to Skathi for protection. I pray to the drowned, because they're my grandfathers, and they know the price the Skagerrak Sea may demand.

Even though these are the first stirrings of summer, there's north wind that seeks out the back of our necks. It fills the sails, but tightens the shoulders for rowing.

Still the gods are either with us, or not against us, and in this as in other things, it's enough. We cross in a day.

It's not joyless, though it is hard going. As the sea falls away from the coast, the swells are a relentless drumbeat, an animal, so each has to be addressed, steered into, rowed through. The wind shifts the width of a palm and the fixtures rattle, ropes creak, the spray makes a rare dry spot damp again, robbing heat. Though there is music, jokes and laughter, gossip. There is a cook who is a master at setting and lifting a pot lid in between waves, a kind of dance to his step of lift, add, stir, taste, set the lid, stoke the coals, lash the pot if necessary. The sky is clear, which makes for an easier crossing but a colder night. The stars are sharp against the carved dragon's head of my own boat.

We don't anchor, but sail through, taking advantage of a hole in the weather. This isn't taxing; the rowers work in shifts, so others sleep in a line along the hull's length, bundled in cloaks and under cow-hide tents.

Dawn wakes me, and I look back to see what we've set loose upon the world. A massive fleet of some ninety ships, though most of these on skeleton crews, the smaller ships unmanned and towed behind. Still, this is nearly the forest of masts of my vision, and it is beautiful as the morning sun burns the mist off the water. No sign of land yet, but the colour of the sea has changed, and we are through the danger of it.

But there is land, the northern tip of the Jutland, and a cheer to greet it. A boat approaches from behind us: Ragnar's skeith.

Our oars are up to allow the boat to come alongside, and Ragnar's long legs clear the gunwales in a smooth lope. He is smiling.

"Good morning, Goat Pants," I say. Someone hands me a bowl of hot broth, and I extend it to him. He shakes his head. "Do we make for Hjorring?" I ask.

"Do we need to?" he asks in reply.

"I don't think so. We're well-provisioned. We could make Aalborg tonight, gather the rest of the ships, take on crew there."

He says nothing for a moment, but cocks his head to the side, as though he'd want us to go for a discreet walk. Those around us take the hint and simply withdraw a pace or two.

"What do you think," he begins, pausing carefully, "Rorik will do when we arrive?"

"What do you mean?" I'm honestly puzzled. The ship creaks and rattles and slaps around us, unhurried.

"So, you expect to sail to your hall and have your ships waiting for you?" Ragnar asks.

"Yes," I have to stop and think for a moment. "Yes, I do."

He nods and shrugs a little, assured.

"You have doubts," I say.

"It was curious that the last time we sailed south together, you and I, that Jarl Rorik was not with us."

"He landed to the north of the fjord, he said," I explained. "He made it to the hall after we did."

"And yet, he was not in the battle." He's stating the obvious, watering the seeds of doubt I've had for months.

"He had meetings with the families north of the town," I explain. Or try to. "He paid them in silver to leave Harald's garrison unsupported."

"This is what he told me as well," says Ragnar.

"You don't believe him," I state.

"I think your husband is very good at counting. And Harald has a great deal of silver for him to count."

"You're suggesting Harald paid Rorik to stay out of the fight?" I should be affecting outrage. This is my husband who's being called a traitor. A coward.

"It's convenient he showed up once he knew how it was all going to turn out," Ragnar says.

I can't deny this.

"So what I'm saying is," Ragnar whispers, "that I will see you in your boats. Even if we have to fight for them."

"Will it come to that?" I honestly wonder.

Again, his typical shrug.

"How would you feel about that, if it does?" he asks.

"About waging war on my husband, you mean? It was your idea that I marry him!"

"Not my best idea," he admits. I expect a smile, but there is none.

"How did you come to know him?" I ask Ragnar. We're sitting on the gunwales now, and I scooch closer to him.

"He owed my father a great deal in taxes," Ragnar explains. "I forgave him that debt when he joined me in killing Fro."

"Makes sense," I say.

"Also, Rorik knows things. He is... cultured. Like the Franks. My world was very small, growing up. Like yours, I guess. But Rorik, Rorik has maps. He can read. He is smart, like a merchant. Their world is larger than ours."

"A world that runs on silver," I say.

"And slaves. There is a river, in the Finnmark, that leads to the center of the world. There is great profit to be made in taking slaves from Anglia and selling them at the rivermouth."

"That doesn't sound like you," I decide.

"No, but controlling the mouth of such a river, taxing it. It is interesting to me."

"And to Rorik, no doubt."

"So we had that in common. But if he thinks Harald can get him there faster than me..." He trails off.

"I understand," I say, and I do. Though I wish I didn't.

"And speaking of slaves," Ragnar says, lightening the mood, "you wear his ring."

I look at the flash of purple glass set in silver on my finger.

"Eindr? No, he says he found it in Rorik's stores, and that it was mine by right."

"It was in Rorik's stores, yes. I was there when he found it, inventorying it. He thought it was fascinating, but it's just glass. Rorik gave it to him."

"The ring was Eindr's?" I ask.

"I think it was the only thing he owned," Ragnar says. "I told you he was in love with you."

As we sail up the Limfjord in the darkness, we leave most of the fleet behind—they sail west and south, well clear of any scouts from the shore. My drakkar is at the head of only a dozen of the ships from the Gaular, just as we are expected to be.

Just in case anything happens.

Ragnar is aboard, at the oars, and cloaked. Not hiding, just not overly visible. I'm the one at the prow, beneath the great carved dragon's head and its snarl, and I'm suddenly aware of the king in my boat. Of the wolf skin around my shoulders. My mother's brooch, the sword at my belt. And the glass ring on my finger bearing the name of an alien god.

Every breath of wind might bring an arrow. I have them light torches to better guide their way. This is my hall by right, by law, and there, ahead of me, the docks and my fleet by troth. No arrow comes.

There are warriors on the dock, wearing leather helms, holding their shields in the night. They don't move to help us with the lines, but they don't murder us either. I begin to wonder why not.

And there in a tunic down to his feet, a silver brocade from throat to hem is Eindr, his eyes downcast.

"Jarl Hladgertha," he says, "welcome home."

Everywhere I go now, everyone says that. How many times can it be true?

It is all my heart can do not to reach out to him, to touch his face. I struggle to find my voice.

"Eindr," I say, with some cobbled-together confidence, "where's Rorik?"

"Jarl Rorik has business, Jarl Hladgertha," he says. "He left this afternoon with some four hundred men on horseback."

"He rides to war?"

"No, Jarl Hladgertha. He merely rides."

"Rides. With a four hundred men."

"As you say, Jarl Hladgertha." His language is stiff. So public. I want to shake him and get my friend back.

"Is it not strange that, Eindr, with enough notice of my return, that he should take off like this? With a small army?" I need to be seen by others saying this.

"Perhaps," he says, "you would like to return to your hall. And we can billet your crew."

I nod, and he smiles and takes a step back before turning.

"Eindr?"

"Jarl Hladgertha?"

"Ragnar is with me. Make preparations for your king."

The girls wake me early. Eindr is waiting outside my house. It is scarcely past dawn and the knots from the voyage have yet to leave my shoulders. But I'm dressed, combed, braided, appointed. Kohl is under my eyes and berries stain my lips, the stain transferring to the thin wooden cup as I sip birch tea.

I go to greet Eindr, who paces to warm himself in the early sun.

"Eindr?" We walk a little for privacy's sake.

"They return, Ladda. Jarl Rorik and his men."

"Thank you, Eindr. Are they here yet?"

"No, but soon. From the east."

I have to think about this for a second. No, I don't, but I should. In the end, I say what I wanted to say since I got here.

"Have my chair brought to the field behind the hall. Set up a pavilion there and bring some wine."

"And chairs for Jarl Rorik and King Ragnar?" he asks.

"My chair and mine alone."

At this, I think he'll just leave. It's difficult to see him, because I don't know where to rest my eyes. Not in the curls of his hair, or the lines of his cheek, the bronze of his hands...

"Ladda? If I may..."

"Of course, Eindr," I answer, grateful for the distraction. Grateful for the break in the uncomfortable silence.

"I have... the timing is odd, but I have something for you. A gift. A welcome-home." And he hands me a fist of green silk, placing it into my waiting palms. "Please be careful, it's sharp."

A spearhead in iron, though the lightest and most silver iron I have ever seen. While made of one piece it seems like a tangle of wires woven together, the work so intricate. As we knot beasts and birds and serpents into our work—yet there are no heads here, no faces. Just a delicate writhing of line and beauty, fragile-seeming yet unbreakable, like something forged by Kara's elves.

"It is Arabic?" I wonder.

"It is. Scripture. A saying. The words make up the spearhead itself."

"Let me guess, you discovered it in inventory and thought it was mine anyway." I'm teasing him. He doesn't know I know about the ring.

Eindr looks left and right, leaning towards me. "Something like that," he says, smiling.

"Thank you, Eindr, it's beautiful." Without thinking I dart forward and kiss him on the cheek. His smile cracks my heart open and I'm amazed to have found it closed so tight.

"I would ask one further gift from you, if you would."

"Anything."

"The truth, then. Did Rorik accept payment from Harald to hold back from retaking Aalborg?"

Eindr says nothing, but in his eyes I can see that he is wounded to have disappointed me. His complete lack of reaction and surprise is all the truth I need from him. I can all but see an iron collar around his throat. I place my hand on his arm.

"Thank you, my friend." I say.

Before the hour's over, I sit attended under a canopy of linen, on the great wooden chair piled high with furs. I can feel the hoofbeats through the grass before I hear them. Ragnar is at the west end of the field, leaning against the back of the hall. I'll say this about my friend: he is beautiful when he leans.

The first riders clear the forest and seem confused. They're not expecting this, me, practically alone in the field at the head of their road. They fan out, allowing Rorik to trot up the center. He looks nervous; his eyes sweep the field. Because I don't rise to greet him, he canters over to me and dismounts.

His feet under him, he dons his most charming smile, and I am reminded how good he is at this. Politics. Business.

"My love," he says, his arms spread wide. "When did you get back?"

"When you saw my ships enter the fjord," I say without emotion. "When you fled."

"We had some business inland," he says. "But what is this?" He gestures to the shade, and the small table set with meats and fruit. And no chair for him. I do not answer. He tries again.

"It is my joy to see you, Ladda. You have no idea how much I've missed you."

"I have some idea," I say, rising.

I do this:

I look at the field where I left a small piece of my ear, the place where I fell in battle from a spear that nearly took my life.

I smell the sweat of horses.

I turn my cheek for a kiss.

I note the green velvet of my husband's Frankish tunic.

I drive the spearpoint in my hand up under his jaw to the small pad of flesh there, pushing again as it crunches against the palette, feel the hot gush of blood staining my hands as he drops gagging and bubbling to his knees at my feet. Dying.

I draw my sword, a thing made for drawing in the sun, so that it whispers itself into my slick hand, and I strike down to his neck, the flecks of blood suddenly raising up my dress to my collarbone, my throat, my face.

I level my sword at four hundred men, still mounted, who are shocked at the murder of their lord by a girl. And there at the centre of all of them is Caldr's scowl.

"Listen to me, all of you," I say. "I have slain the traitor Rorik, in accordance with the law. I and I alone am Jarl of Aalborg. Follow me, and swear me your feal, and I will make you rich. But betray me, or conspire against me again, and you will meet the same fate as this corpse here."

The men look amongst themselves but I try not to notice. One of them could spear me, spear Ragnar, and that would be the end of the war. So simple, really.

None move.

"And you, Caldr," I yell out. "You are free to do one thing and that is ride to Harald, if he will have you. I will not. From this moment you are a wolf's-head in the Jutland, and anyone can kill you if they wish without penalty of law."

A hundred heads turn to Ragnar, unarmed, who continues to lean against the back of the building. He shrugs, but in a comical way, his palms upturned to the heavens. The men laugh, many dismounting to kneel before their Jarl.

Caldr glares at me, but he knows he's done. A single pace towards me and he'll not live another breath. He sneers, as only a man with so much practice at sneering can do, and turns his horse back to the forest. Two men follow, silently, whether to accept him as master or quarry I don't know and don't care.

"Jarl Ladda!" cries one of the kneeling warriors. He calls me by my family name, simpler, and it speaks to kinship.

"Jarl Ladda!" cries another. And this they chant. The serving girls laugh, not knowing if they would share my fate had things gone differently, and now all that nervousness lost to laughter and the pouring of wine. Casks of ale are rolled uphill and bashed open, the men plunging drinking-horns and already singing. The horses, overwhelmed by all the sudden noise, defecate steadily on the grass, and at this the men laugh louder, like children.

Two men come to move Rorik's body.

"No, leave him there," I command. "He will not enter Valhalla."

It's a quiet curse, but a lasting one—there's no way to take back such a thing. The men are horrified. I regret it at once, but can't show it.

"Eindr!" I shout, though it seems he is right behind me. Of course he is.

"Ladda?" He'd dig out that spearhead from Rorik's throat and throw himself on it if I asked him to.

"It's in my power to free you, now," I say. I'm guessing, but I'm pretty sure I'm right.

"Free me?" He doesn't understand, at first.

"From thrall. You're not a slave, anymore, Eindr. You're whatever you want to be."

He swallows. "There's only one thing I want to be," he says.

"Then be that."

And so I kiss him, the blood from my hand in his hair, but we don't care and all the world is watching and his mouth is on mine and he's strong, so much stronger in his arms than I thought it would be, and there's only him and the scent of him and the pounding of my heart. There is cheering because a heartbeat ago there was uncertainty and now there is not. Now there is only their Ladda and her consort Eindr and that is a simple enough thing for anyone to understand. Something even my heart can understand.

I take my lover's hand and practically march to my house, by the hall.

"And where are you going, Jarl Ladda?" asks Ragnar as we pass. He hasn't moved from his spot, but his happiness for me, the smile on his face, is priceless.

"Mind your own business, Goat Pants," I say, not stopping.

I allow myself two days.

Two days.

All business can fall to Ragnar. Eindr and I don't leave our bed. We have food, water, wine brought to us. All there is of us is love. Skin. Hunger. Sleep. The days are for love, and for drifting in and out of dreams. Nights are for sharing, for whispering to one another. Childhood stories. Secrets. Incidents written into our flesh by fine scars. He kisses my ragged ear. I kiss his neck where there are marks from an iron collar in his boyhood.

He thinks I'm the goddess Thorgertha. He worships me like one, in an instant, then teases me in the next. We're drunk on one another and the places we inhabit in each other's hearts.

No one interrupts us. I just know, on waking on the third dawn, that it is time.

He's still asleep when I steal from our bed, and I leave the curtained dormer and rouse the two dressing-girls. They tend to the fire and the kettle, and my hair is unbraided, combed, and oiled, rebraided.

Eindr stands naked by the curtain, watching me dress. He wants to ask me to come back. I want him to ask me. But I can't, so he'll say nothing. He knows, too. He gets dressed.

We hold hands as we walk down to the docks together, the morning wind in the rigging of a hundred and twenty ships. A fleet like the sea has never known.

Ragnar has been busy. Many have been sleeping aboard, and the docks are piled high with barrels, bundles, weapons, casks, great jars sealed with wax. It's a market-smell of dried fish and copper, though it's not a market we sail to.

"It's all right," Eindr says, "I know we'll have to sail soon. Today, if you like."

My throat is a bottle found in a barn, empty and hollow and dusty.

"What is it? What's wrong?" he asks. "Everything will be perfect so long as we're together."

"Eindr," I say, holding both his hands in mine. "You can't come with me."

"Of course I can."

"You can't. I need you not to."

He still doesn't believe me.

"It will be fine, Ladda," he says.

"It will. But not like this. I need you to go." This is impossible for me. I am breaking my own heart.

"Go? Go where? I'm not leaving your side," he insists.

"Stop. Just stop, please? Listen?" I kiss his fingers, because if he wipes the tears from my cheeks I won't be able to do this. "I'm sending you to the Nordvegr. To be the jarl of the Gaular."

He tries to interrupt, but a simple "please" silences him. I continue.

"You're the only one I trust. I'm giving you the Gaular. It's mine, and I'm giving it to you because I believe in you, in your strength and your learning. You can make something of the place, something important. And you'll have Kara and Brandr..."

"I don't need Kara and Brandr," he says. "I need you."

"You have me. Oh my gods, you have me. And we'll be together, I swear it. But I need to know that the Gaular is safe, that my sister is safe and that my people won't just fade away if..."

"Don't speak like that. Nothing's going to happen."

"Still. I need you there. They need you. You need to speak with Kara, have her teach you the runes she taught me. You need to figure out how we can teach them to others. Skalds, I mean. Our runes, they're... special. Different. Your learning... just... figure it out." I'm babbling. "Please, Eindr. For me. Go and build something."

He knows it's decided and that all of him wants to fight me. I want him to fight me. I want him to win, to ignore me and stay by my side every second.

But we both know it can't be like that.

"I'm sending you north with seven ships," I tell him. "With blacksmiths and quarrymen, and enough iron to build a fortress. You'll find a garrison, not just warriors but families, who will settle and fight for the Gaulardale."

"That's three hundred people, Ladda," he says. "Dozens of families. Think of what that will do to Aalborg. That's your responsibility, too."

"Take some from Aalborg, some from Hjorring. Villages in between, or just offer," I tell him. "Take livestock, cattle, sheep, horses, anything you might need. Tools and weapons. Make it strong. Make it beautiful. Build stone halls. And then I'll come and stay with you. Forever. I promise."

A dockside gift from Ragnar—I don't know how or when he conceived of this or managed to make it all happen.

"There are privileges to being king," he says when I ask. "You'd like it."

And on every mast a banner in red with a swan emblazoned in white. The Swanfleet of my dream, real, and here bobbing in the harbour. I don't know how many hours, how much thread, how many beats of the loom this must have taken. The banners glint with fine silver wire woven into the design to catch the light, over and over, flashing with the breeze.

The priests here wanted a blot, a sacrifice of some dozen swans. I forbade it. Let them kill something we can eat, I tell them. So, what would be blasphemy is credited to practicality.

The wind comes off the land as the tide goes out, and we cruise through the Limfjord to the west with spacing our largest issue: wind and water want us all to collide in a clump, and the rocks here too unforgiving for such closeness. Half the ships are loosely cabled together on long lines, so that those closest to shore can be given a few extra backs for maneuvering as needed.

Once clear of the shore, we're greeted by almost a dozen ships belonging to those loyal to Ragnar. Set out from Heithabyr and following the coastline, there's been no sign of Harald between the isle of Fyn and the Jutland. He is somewhere out in the Kattegat. There is some debate whether to return to the fjord, past Aalborg, and so take the eastern passage to the sea.

Hearing this nearly kills me. There's no way I can turn around and sail past Aalborg, past Eindr. There's no way I can say goodbye again, no way not to stop and either throw my arms around him or throw myself into the waves. I can have war. But I can't bear the thought of this.

But Ragnar decides, and mercifully we are to take the long way around. So for us it's north, around the northernmost spits, and then south to the straits between Fyn and Sjeland. From there we can resupply at Roskilde, and cross to Lund if necessary.

All these names, shapes of islands drawn in the dust. We have to know these waters, understand them, or die.

If Harald is running, we give him an advantage with our numbers, being so easy to spot from shore. But if he stands and fights, it's a navy we kill him with.

The journey north is hard, as the wind is fickle and we are oars against the tide. But our backs are fresh, and there's no rain, and this is the part of war that has every boy looking as joyous as serious. No enemy in sight, but the world of spear and shield, and new songs, and bawdy jokes, camaraderie and abundant fresh water for thirst. The new boys haven't heard the stories a hundred times, have never seen their brothers bleed out whimpering on their laps.

Not yet.

Ashore, for a Thing with the captains. There are so many of us it takes nearly an hour for the ships to move out of the way to allow the rowboats to beach. Here, there are great cooking fires, debts settled, gear hauled out and repaired, traded.

I don't see Rota so much as know. I just... *know*. And I turn and Rota is there, under a stiff leather cap and broad in shoulder, a rower's shoulders.

"Rota!" I cry, and my arms are around the scent of the sea, the scent of war. Sweat, leather, copper rivets. Smoke and salt and dried fish.

"Ladda," Rota says, voice muffled by the kissing of cheeks and my barrage of affection, and I'm half-lifted off the ground.

"Kara told me you were dead," I say, still trying to catch my breath.

"Almost," Rota says. "Probably close enough for the gods to say so. And you?"

"Almost." There's a respectful beat of silence between us, even though we're still tangled in each other's arms. "Let me look at you."

There is the conspirator of my childhood there still, somewhere under the sun-baked skin and ragged hair. The eyes are older, decades older, but there is the familiar solidity, the strength. Conviction. A confidence in fate which I lack.

"Did you take a wife, as Gudrun said?" I ask.

"A wife! We're not all as old as you, Ladda. Of course, I know you're a legend now."

"I've gotten pretty good at shutting people up," I tease.

"Apparently not. They say you're either Alfhild the Pirate Queen, thrown out of Hel and the sea, or the goddess Thorgertha herself. You can turn yourself into a swan."

"How much ale went into reaching that conclusion?" I ask.

Rota grins. "Word from the Gaular?"

"Fine. Better than fine. There is a new jarl, Eindr, you might remember him. He is..." I break off.

"You're in love with him," Rota says.

"That was... yes. How did you know?"

"The way you said his name," and this followed by laughter, "I thought you married that fop from Aalborg?"

"He died," I answer sternly.

"I'm sorry," Rota says.

"I helped. A little."

Rota laughs louder, pounds me on the shoulder, which makes me wince with pain I'd forgotten. "So, not sorry then! Come, let's find some ale."

"No time," I sigh. "I have to attend the Thing."

Rota mocks me with a bow. "Certainly, Jarl Hladgertha." And with that, as Rota turns, I feel a sharp smack on my bum.

"Brat!" I shout, laughing.

Gods. When you are not hauling fate and love around as though they were toys, what must you do?

We're just sailing.

How many mils under the hulls of boats have I known in my seventeen years? And all together with my crew, the Swanfleet? Back to the dawn of the gods. Back to Ginungagap.

There's a voice rising in the back of my throat. Maybe my mother's voice. Maybe Kara's. Maybe my own. But it rings out to the crew.

"It sates itself on the life-blood of fated men, paints the homes of the gods crimson with blood, and the sun's beams grow black. All the summers that follow become winter. Do you still seek to know?"

And there are cheers, or nods, at the old story. The Darkening of the Gods.

"Brothers will fight and slay one another, and sister's children will deny kinship. A harshness in the world, of axes and swords and shields riven. An age of wind and wolf, before the world goes headlong without mercy."

"Yggdrasil the Tree of All Worlds shudders, and Jormungaddr, the Serpent Under the World, roils and thrashes, with great waves across all the seas. The giants of Jotunheim walk again, their dwarf-servants opening the doors to Asgard. Odinn himself falls before the jaws of the great wolf, Fenrir. But Vidthar, Odinn's son, takes revenge and splits the jaws of the wolf open, even as Thor falls in battle over the slain serpent. The age of the gods is over, and the sea covers all Midgard, with every fire from every hearth hissing into the air."

In my mind I draw the runes upon them. *R* for raiding and riding and reigning, the spokes of a chariot wheel. *A* is the ash-tree, Yggdrasil itself, upon whose branches all worlds hang. *G* the gift, or that which is given, granted. *N* for need. An *A* again, returning to the tree and back to *R* for symmetry. But then *O* for owning, for owing, and finally *K* for kindling, the burning brand of fire and fear and finality, charring all that remains.

Ragnarok.

The crew are grim. As the words are meant to make them. Forge them. Sharpen them.

"And this fate, this *orleg*, we bring to Harald!" I'm shouting now, the growl of the audience rising as their blood comes up.

"His false kingdom is that of the black sun and dying powers. His jaws crack open and hang limp as Vidthar's spears shall make them!"

They're roaring now, men and women and boys, banging fists against shields, boots agains the hull, and the sea is a reverberation.

A warning to the dead, and those who will soon join them.

At first, it's an island. And then it isn't.

Some thirty, forty ships, lashed tightly together in the middle of the Kattegat Sea. Harald's kingdom, then, with no land beneath him. He's made his own.

Ragnar's ship doesn't signal, it just rows like Hel eastward into the midst of it, and the rest are expected to follow. I'm not so sure.

I signal to my flank to break away. There's little wind, but such as it is it would take us south, so sails are lowered and we row hard north. I want to see this thing before we attack it.

We can make out the crew, and there are fifteen hundred warriors at once, on any flank we choose to attack. Clever. The first boat to attack would be overwhelmed. And the second. Ragnar and those immediately behind him run headlong. The sea begins to be peppered with the arrows of the impatient.

But to the south, another flotilla. Faster, smaller ships. Not the busse which make up the bulk of the island but skeiths with a rigging I've never seen before.

Not rigging. Some kind of device. Twenty? No, thirty of them. Half Harald's fleet, looking to trap us between the device-ships and the floating island.

And now I see the reason of it. The timbers from the smaller ships, all with their sails down, seem to explode in action of beam and rope and fire. Great arcs of flaming balls reach out almost lazily to Ragnar's ships, hissing and choking in the ocean.

Greek fire.

Should even one of these missiles strike a target, each boat is lost, and forty rowers clad in mail will be dragged to the green of the Kattegat Sea.

Ragnar has stopped short. He's matching Harald's tactics of lashing boats together, so that a boarding party might have not forty warriors but a hundred. But this slows them down, and each second brings them an oar stroke closer to the reach of Harald's fire-ships.

The first screams of those felled by arrows. Fire-arrows lance out from Harald's island, though none are returned. Ragnar means to board, and there is nothing to be gained from boarding a burning ship, let alone thirty.

We're already out of range of the fire ships, so our only course is south and east, to come around behind the island and open a second flank.

The sky itself seems to catch fire. The boats in behind Ragnar's train are hit, and crews try desperately to chop away flaming boards just as they're drenched with seawater. The rowboats in tow are dragged in, the more experienced already thinking of an escape from the flames that doesn't involve drowning.

But another erupts, and another.

The wind takes barked commands and the screams of the burning to our ears.

"Hold!" I yell. "Oars up!"

The crew obeys, but they're confused. It looks like hesitation. Like fear, maybe, and I can't deny the fear that claws at my gut and makes my throat ache to retching. But I wait.

"Harald," I address the great raft quietly, "Pretender. Unclean thing reviled by the gods, I come for you. Like fish guts left for gulls, I shall leave you. From every wind in Midgard, I curse you."

In the air I trace the runes for need, for hail. Cursing chaos against the foe.

Ragnar has some six or seven ships lashed together, and this ungainly creature is rowing one side only to get a boarding angle onto Harald's ships. The wooden island lurches as hundreds of waiting warriors scramble ship to ship to form a disciplined shield wall: archers, shields and axes, spears at the back.

"Harald," I chant, louder this time. "Fro has fallen before my curses, and so I curse you. No hall shall welcome you. The drowned call to you. Your spear shaft breaks and your manhood withers. Your shield shatters as you piss down your leg in fear. I curse you. I curse you. I curse you!"

I throw something, out of intuition, some invisible ball of malice and spite and hatred, borne by wind and my own need, my own hunger, to see Harald's men fall.

"Now!" I cry and our archers can just barely take out a few of their spears from behind. We're only a few lengths away from the enemy, and their lines are starting to form against us. But still, there is confusion. They expected us to either surround them first, or to bet everything on a single front. Not a concentrated attack on two fronts.

Closer and closer. The ships groan. The blades of the oars in the water, and I think of my father carving such oars, almost idly, lost in the scent of the wood and its beauty, the shavings curling away from the tool-blade making little spiraling waves of their own.

A loud chunk shakes me from this, brings me back to the present. A throwing axe, well below its target, which I realize was me. I don't bother to pluck it from my shield.

I hold up my fist. This signals half the rowers to reverse, pulling my drakkar alongside, so close their spear tips are over our gunwales. But none move until I give the order. A few spears are teased by the longer of our axes.

And then they board us.

They roar and howl and curse and leap; their shield wall pushes against our own as they clamber over the sides, blinded by their own hunger for our deaths.

What they don't do is think.

Another signal, and our oars push us off, trapping some twenty of their warriors aboard, suddenly outnumbered, as another dozen of their fellows are dragged into the gap between boats, already racing to the sea-floor, still alive but simply waiting in their horror to drown.

My warriors cut down the panicking enemy first, those who look back or dart around for a way to escape. There is none. Those who remain are determined to die killing as many as possible, and the solution is patience, restraint, withdrawal.

We have none of this, so the whole thing is a gory mess of a fight, fists and axes and shield-rims crashing and crunching and butchering. But the thing is over, and I signal and scream over the sounds of battle to return to the oars. We go again.

There are no arrows at all from them now, all their archers at the west end of the battle, keeping Ragnar at bay. My fist up, our oars up, and again we wait until they board, we push off, their men once more encircled and trapped, the clumsy falling into the ravenous, insatiable sea. And we slaughter them.

I look up, and one of Harald's own fireships is itself engulfed in glorious flame, whatever cursed fuel the thing needs having exploded and devouring crew and hull and sky. The fire rumbles like an avalanche, and I see a giant in the flames. A thing from Muspelheim, the *eldjotnr*; the fire giants. Only at Ragnarok, at the end of all worlds, are such things meant to walk in Midgard. Yet here they are.

And they are marching upon us.

The fire-boat, adrift, meanders towards us with each bob of what's left of its hull.

"Prepare to board!" I yell, and I don't know who can hear me over all of this, but a single raised sword seems to do the trick. Bows are stowed under seats, long boarding axes grabbed, shields up, oars down, and may the gods be with us, or blind to us.

Half Harald's men are in panic either due to the oncoming fire-giants or to the collapsing shield wall under Ragnar's attack. And we are coming, two hundred of us, near-tripping over the churning platform of boats right behind their line. My shield fowls on the rigging of the next boat, and I drop it, not taking my eyes off the battle. I don't care. I think we'll all die when the *eldjotnr* come for us, and I have work to do yet.

My sword is its own thing now, made only for this. Exposed backs, and the backs of necks, the soft hollow of the knee. The joint of a wrist so soon gone from an arm, and a weapon with it. And as their line turns to us, now in the thick of it their spearmen are targets for Ragnar's own spears, so we hammer them between us, every slice and spatter and gasp bringing us closer not to victory but to the immolation that waits for us.

And then everyone is gone.

Simply gone.

I'm alone, on a tightly-bound island of close-woven ships. Not a blood-drop for all my efforts. No enemy, no crew, no soul in all of Midgard. The fire ship seems to have halted in its progress but not in its burning. The light, I realize, is strangely beautiful.

A shadow flashes over my face—a single white swan flying between me and the sun. I watch her arc slowly, elegantly, with minimal effort, around and to the south, where her wings begin to beat steadily, carrying her towards Sjeland.

In the boat-lengths between the raft and the fire-ship, she stands on the sea-foam.

"Do you expect me to kneel?" I call to the goddess.

"Never," says Skathi.

She steps toward the flames, reaches out to touch them gently, like flowers. They are almost solid to her, tangible as rushing water, and they do not burn her. Her hand reaches along the keel lovingly— yes, that makes sense, I think, the tide goddess must feel the kiss of every keel on the ocean—and pushes it up, so that the whole ship arches up and back, its stern taking on water in a thundering hiss of steam.

"Just remember: I am the tide. I give you this gift," she gestures to the drowning ship, "and I take. I always take. It is what I am."

"What are you taking from me? Am I dying?"

"You're not drowning. That much I know."

"So what are you taking from me?" I repeat in frustration, and fear.

"I already have him."

Eindr.

I know it's Eindr. And something else, too, something I can't see in the rush of my rage and grief.

"What? Why? Why would you drown Eindr? How has he... how have I ever done anything that you didn't ask of me?"

"It's I who have done what you asked, Ladda. I'm still doing it," says the goddess.

She turns to me.

"Ladda?" she says, and then there are thousands of us, dying, killing, wounded and wounding, on a wooden island that seems almost silly now, the weight of us pushing the boats down, down into the sea, the water merely a palm's width beneath the sides.

Reflexively I parry an axe with my sword, step back and swipe at a nose that comes off almost accidentally. A warrior steps back into me and we both stumble and fall, his weight knocking the wind from me and I'm gasping, the small of my back into something hard, bruising, cold. I try to yell at him to get off me, but I have no voice in my lungs and besides the man is dead with not much skull remaining to hear me with.

I try to untwist my left arm from beneath me, but the shoulder is either broken or the nerve severed; it won't move. I notice the corpse's mail, and it is unusually fine. A treasure, in fact, I could claim if I can ever get the damn weight off me. And beneath the mail a tunic, not the coarse wool of a rower, but a thing of linen and silk. A tunic for a king, or a pretender king.

Harald. Dead here across my gasping chest. He weighs the same as a barn, pinning me to the deck, immobile.

It's all I can do to turn my head and watch the fire ship slip backwards into the Kattegat Sea, harmless and well clear of us.

The killing lasts another hour. No one gets around to killing me.

The pain in my shoulder is trying to, however. And I need to pee. This fact would get me laughing if I had the air for it, but it's all I can do to gasp enough to stay alive.

I'm found, or rather, Harald is found, and the woman with the gore-choked axe is as delighted by her prize as she is startled to find me alive under it. Every other warrior joins in the finding, until Harald's name is an echo that hangs snagged in the columns of masts.

I am hauled to my feet, an act that nearly causes me to black out. The woman who finds me is practical enough to know that I'll vouch for her discovery, the reward hers by right, and she sees to my shoulder by moving me away from the shield boss on which I've been lying, placing me on the flat deck, and putting her foot in my armpit. She pulls my wrist with strength and certainty, and on releasing it my arm is once again in its socket, though it sings a little song of crunching flesh that the day has found popular and got stuck in its head.

I scream and nearly vomit. I'm not sure why I don't.

She takes my belt, a fine thing of Kara's weaving, and binds my wrist between my breasts. Another quick sash under my elbow and the weight of the arm is off altogether. I'm too dizzy, too much in shock to thank her when she hands me my sword.

"Jarl Ladda," she nods, and turns to drag Harald's body in Ragnar's direction.

On Ragnar's confirmation, there is a cheer almost as loud as the roaring of fire giants. He seeks me out.

"Are you all right?" His face is elation.

"I've been lying under your friend there for an hour," I tell him. "And I need to pee."

He laughs. "I'll find you a bucket."

"Over the gunwales for me," I say sickly. "I am the boatbuilder's daughter."

"Ladda," says Ragnar, serious now, "I could not have taken this without you."

"I know, Goat Pants," I answer. "I know."

Ashore at Sjeland, there is a familiar *knowing*, here among the joyous, the arguing, the trading. Among the dead.

Rota.

Rota's leather cap is still atop ragged hair, now red, now brown and matted with blood in the sun. Freckles I used to count each summer, contrasted against a skin the green-grey of fish. Of the drowned.

Of Eindr's, too, I remember.

"You went off to war, as you said you would," I tell Rota's body. I would cry, but there is nothing in me. Nothing at all. I want to fall to my knees in rage and mourning, but instead I kneel beside the corpse purposefully, slowly.

"And you took Skathi for your bride, just as Gudrun said you would take a wife. Young as you are."

Were, part of me corrected. *She warned she would take you.*

Where in Hel are the Valkyries? I want them here, demand them. Not in fever-dream, but real, their wings beating the fading blue of the sky. I want to hear them singing as they carry my kin to the halls of our ancestors. I'm in no mood for poetry. I want the meat of these flying women before me. Something real I can touch, or weep upon, or strike out in rage.

They owe me enough to be real.

My right hand wants to move, to touch the cold face, to brush the salt-wet hair. But I don't move. I'm not sad. Not angry. I'm just hollow at the sight of Rota.

Blank. Accepting. Like that day on the beach.

All done.

All done.

Except for the singing.

It comes from a great distance, muffled by the wind, so that I can't place the tune, though it's familiar. Increasingly and hauntingly so. Something my mother used to sing, in a language I only half know.

A song in my own voice.

And the song gives my hand movement, so that I can close Rota's mouth and feel the cool skin against my fingertips; so that I can lean down and kiss the forehead, which stops the song for just an instant, but it resumes as I come up and set the body just so.

And by sunset I am still singing this song, though now I stand on a hilltop on an island well south of any home I have claim to, as warriors light pyres to a sky growing dark pink in the west.

"Wait," I whisper, and it's enough for the honour guard to hear me. "Wait."

I step closer to Rota, laying across the stout beams, strong as the arms that protected me, shielded me, even when I was the older sister. I draw my sword, beautiful and lithe, and place it lengthwise along the unbreathing chest. And I want Eindr here with me, even though he's down there in the sea watching us in in the grey-green light and not holding my hand, and I want to kiss Kara's forehead and tell her everything will be all right forever now, that we will survive and our people will not fade and our runes will last and no winter can erase us now.

Because we're strong, and we've paid every price, and we've won everything now. And we have nowhere to go, not even to our deaths anymore. We can't be forgotten, because all of forgetting is full and will not take us. So, we stay. Survive. Endure.

Remembered.

I step back, and nod, and watch until the sparks from the fire become the glints of stars, and the song is no longer in my throat.

"To the Galaurdale, then?" asks Ragnar.

We're sharing a rock on this beach, as the tents are hammered around us, and weary rowers attend ropes, wounds. Rowboats scrape ashore against tumbled rocks, and the wind's come up. The beach is a chorus of fires in the night, stretching along the shore in both directions around the bay.

I don't answer for a moment, so he continues. He's just filling up space, but he's not saying he'll miss me. Which he will.

"You're very rich now, you know," he says. "Richer than you realize. Eindr can tell you. You have enough silver to turn your village into Hjorring. Into Aalborg."

"Eindr is dead," I say calmly.

"I'm sorry," Ragnar says. "How do you know?"

"My sister would say a swan turned into a goddess and told me before sinking Harald's fire-ships."

He nods. "That is a lot to know." Again, he kicks the pebbles on the beach.

"I am divorcing Thora," he adds.

"What? Why?" This makes no sense to me. "She's a good queen."

Again, he nods at the fact of it. "It's true. But she wants me in the south, in the hall. To be king."

"And you don't want that?"

He shrugs. "I want to be with you. Out here. Simple."

"This is not so simple, Ragnar," I tell him.

"She can stay where she is as jarl. I'll pay her to keep the city. All of Harald's lands are mine now. Silver, too. Contracts. She'll be rich. Richer than she is now. Her family will like that. There's no loss to her."

"But she loves you."

"No, but we trust each other. And I'll take care of her. She won't mind."

"So that's your plan? Now that you're the king of the Nordvegr and Jutland and Sjeland and all the Kattegat Sea? Divorce?"

"That's my plan, yes," he says.

"And the Swanfleet?" I ask. "What is to become of it?" I pick up a pebble from the beach, toss it in my palm, and arc it high into the water.

"What do you want? You won't need a hundred ships in the Gaular. The war is over."

He bends to the shore to find a stone for himself. So we talk like children, and not of fortunes.

"A hundred and twenty," I say. "A hundred and fifty, perhaps, once Harald's ships are repaired." *Plonk.* A fragment of earth, returned to the tide.

"Midgard has never seen such a fleet," he says, approvingly. His arm is strong and his stone sails high and far, so far the sound of its falling is muted.

"Let's say a hundred and fifty ships, then. Five thousand warriors," I say.

"Faster than any army in the world. Up river, deep inland, down the coast, across the sea. Anywhere," he agrees.

"You could take the mouth of the Finnmark," I tell him, the toe of my boot idly searching for another rock.

"Or the entire coast of Anglia." He's thinking. Raids of Christian gold like the times of our grandfathers.

"Or the Seax, to the south, who would never harry the Jutland again," I remember, hearing this from Eindr.

"Or you could just go home," he says. He smiles a little at this. Daring me.

"I could. I will, in fact." And there's some stubbornness in my voice, challenging him to push me further.

"Good. Good," Ragnar nods. "You should do that."

"I will," I say, tossing the stone in the palm of my one unbound arm, feeling the salt rub on my skin.

"Good," he repeats. "Go home."

When he leans in to kiss me, my mouth is already open for him, my hand on his strong jaw and his hands in my hair, the taste of the salt air on his lips and woodsmoke on his skin, and my chest expands in breath and heartbeats until I could moor the entire fleet in there. And just as quickly, he stops, though he takes my hand.

"And the Frankish capitol?" I ask. "How far is that? From here?"

"Paris? The richest place in all the world. Where they spend gold as we spend copper," he says. "Three days?" He thinks for a moment, nodding. "Three days."

"Three days," I say, tossing the stone. *Plonk.*

"Interesting."

And we both smile in the night's breeze, knowing.

FIN

ABOUT THE AUTHOR

Jordan Stratford has been pronounced clinically dead, and was briefly (mistakenly) wanted by INTERPOL for international industrial espionage. He has won numerous sword fights, jaywalked the streets of Paris, San Francisco, and São Paulo, and was once shot by a stray rubber bullet in a London riot. He lives in the crumbling colonial capital of a windswept Pacific island, populated predominantly by octogenarians and carnivorous gulls.

He has been featured on c/net, io9, boingboing, WIRED, and Reading Rainbow and is represented by Silvia Molteni at Peters, Fraser + Dunlop in London.